So You're Still Having a Bad Day?

THREE MORE STORIES
TO MAKE YOU FEEL BETTER!

Matthew Braga

SO YOU'RE STILL HAVING A BAD DAY?
THREE MORE STORIES TO MAKE YOU FEEL BETTER!

This is a work of fiction. All of the characters, names, incidents, organizations, and dialogue in this novel are either the products of the author's imagination or are used fictitiously.

iUniverse books may be ordered through booksellers or by contacting:

iUniverse
1663 Liberty Drive
Bloomington, IN 47403
www.iuniverse.com
1-800-Authors (1-800-288-4677)

ISBN: 978-1-4917-5801-4 (sc)
ISBN: 978-1-4917-5800-7 (e)

Library of Congress Control Number: 2015902067

Print information available on the last page.

iUniverse rev. date: 10/21/2015

CONTENTS

ACKNOWLEDGMENTS

I would like to thank my wife for her patience and understanding for a second book.

Thanks to my mom for the pictures, review, and input... again.

Thanks to Kumo for the technical advice; it was great.

Thanks to my friend Justine for her review and input.

And thanks to Emmy, who helped start "When the Weather Cries."

INTRODUCTION

My name is Matthew Braga, and I am a retired US Navy Seabee. I have been writing short stories for about ten years. It wasn't until about a year and a half ago that one of my friends suggested I try publishing one or more of them. I thought, *Who would read these stories?* I shared them with a few more people and got some real compliments. I never thought of myself as a writer, but I have been known to tell a few stories. I received an advertisement from this company, iUniverse, to publish my stories. Less than a year later, my first book, *So You Think You're Having a Bad Day?*, was published, sharing four short and humorous stories about four different people having a "bad day." My mom says, "If you think you're having a bad day, call a relative or friend. There's always someone with more problems than you."

In this book, you will find three more people with problems of their own. The problems are a little different from the ones I wrote about in my first book but are problems nonetheless.

In the first story we meet Sean, a writer who has a story he really wants to tell—if he can get it past his editor. It's a murder mystery that he has wanted to tell for a long time, and now feels he must tell it. Will it get published, or will the editor just "round file" it?

In the second story we meet Mr. Stanley, a construction site safety officer, a man who is happily married and has three children but who has always dreamed about what life would have been like if he had chosen a different path. He is about to find out as he tests the resilience of the human body.

And in the third story, we meet Mark, a construction worker with a memory problem from a childhood accident. He lives in a small Pennsylvanian town with a sheriff who wants to go big time. It's a story based on the old adage "He who spends all his time searching for conspiracy will eventually find it."

These stories are just that—stories. Using my imagination to spin a yarn or two. It helps me pass the time away as I travel for work.

I now tell everyone who asks me how I got started, "Everyone has a story to tell. Just write about it."

Hope you enjoy.

WHEN THE WEATHER CRIES

Prologue

I n a small office on the second floor of the public building, the window was halfway open, and a soft afternoon breeze slowly moved the curtains. The smell of fresh-cut grass floated in from somewhere down the block, just out of range of the lawnmower running at a feverish pace in the hot afternoon sun.

Sitting at the desk, with papers piled waist-high, was Mr. Robert T. Snelson, editor in chief of the Baxter Book Company on the East Coast (the title of which was written on the glass door to his office). The walls were half-papered with a light-blue-and-white striping and had certificates and letters of appreciation from various stores and now famous writers. The bottom half of the wall was a medium-light-brown wood-grained panel.

Robert was pushing forty, was average height, had a thick-rimmed pair of glasses sliding down the sweat on the bridge of his nose, was a little overweight, and was balding on the top of his head. His black hair was thick around the sides and back of his head, and he sported a very thick mustache.

Whether he was reading or typing, a cigarette perpetually stuck out of the side of his mouth. He drank his coffee out of his favorite cup, one his wife had given him one year for

Christmas as a joke, which read, "Yes, I am the *BOSS*. Any *more* silly questions?" on the side in big, bold blue letters.

*

From across town, Sean carried his briefcase to his one o'clock meeting. In the heat of the day, it seemed Sean was losing steam the closer he got to his destination—or was it something else? He stopped at the front door to the building and took a deep breath before reaching out for the handle. He picked up his pace and headed up the stairs. Sean walked in at 12:55. Robert looked up through his glasses as he slid them back into place. Sean immediately thought of a cartoon character with big bug eyes.

Robert leaned back in his chair, looked at the clock on the wall, and said out of the side of his mouth, "You're early! That's a good sign. Sit down, sit down. Want some coffee? I made it about fifteen minutes ago." He paused and then mumbled, looking down at his own cup, said, "I think I made it fifteen minutes ago."

Sean looked around for a seat, spotted a chair, and had to pick up the pile of paper from it. He looked around for a place to put the papers and decided on the floor, next to another pile of papers. As he sat down, he placed the briefcase on his lap and said with a half smile, "No, no, thanks, really. I just came from lunch over at the diner. They really do have a great lunch. You should get out more often. You look … I don't know … tired."

"*Holy cow!* Not you too? Hey, that's why I have a wife. You're supposed to be the writer, not my mother." He paused just long enough to switch from anger to almost calm. "And speaking of which, is that it—the finished copy?" he asked with a smile from ear to ear as ash from his cigarette fell onto the desk.

Sean first looked out the window, watching the breeze blow the trees across the street. He glanced at the briefcase on his lap and, without looking up, said in almost a whisper, "Yeah, I guess so."

"Well, is it or isn't it? Are you going to let me read it or what?" And kind of offhandedly, he said, "I hope it's better than your last couple of stories."

Still looking down, Sean said, "I think you're going to like this one. I really do." Sean stood up, turned around, and placed his briefcase on the empty chair. He opened it and took out a thick folder and handed it to Robert.

"Wow, it's pretty thick," Robert said as his smile slowly left his face. "How long did it take to write this one?"

"Not as long as I thought it might. Go ahead. Take your time. I really want to know what you think. Be honest."

"Ha-ha, ain't I always?"

Sean smiled and turned back around. He closed and picked up his briefcase, looked out the window, and said, "Yeah, I guess you always have been. That breeze feels good. I think I'll do some shopping in town. I'll be around, if you have any questions. I'll talk to you later."

Sean opened the door and looked back at Robert one more time, who was still looking at the folder in his hands. Sean looked left toward the staircase to head down to the ground floor but stopped. Quietly he said, "I mean it. I really want to know what you think about this one. It's … it's really important."

Opening the folder and not looking up, Robert said, "Yeah, yeah. Be honest. I will, I will." Robert took a sip of his coffee, lit another cigarette, and turned to the first page in the folder and began to read.

Sean smiled a little, closed the door, and started for the stairs.

CHAPTER 1

Someone once wrote, "Life is like wrestling a gorilla. You don't stop when *you* get tired; you stop when the *gorilla* gets tired." Most of the time life is exhausting enough, and then you have a really rough day to make the others seem … easy.

Let's take the life of Bobby Smith, for instance. Bobby has a good nine-to-five job, lives alone, and, like most people, has a pet. True, fish don't take up much of your time—you don't pet them or take them out for walks or have to let them in at night. However, they are soothing to watch. They don't complain, they don't leave hair all over the furniture, and they don't play with messy toys that you step on in the middle of the night. They just swim back and forth. A little food and they're happy. If only our lives could be so easygoing sometimes.

I'm sure Bobby would have wished that on one particular summer day, not so long ago.

Bobby had a desk in front of a window, and to him, it made the office seem not as small as it really was for the ten people who worked in this part of the building. Every day Bobby got to work about fifteen minutes early to grab a cup of coffee from the deli around the corner (where he got a good deal and the coffee tasted better than at work).

He sipped it slowly and watched the traffic on 95 from his fourth story, half-walled cubicle office. He didn't like being able to see everyone else, but for the first fifteen minutes, it was only him and sometimes a couple other people.

One rainy summer day, while drinking his coffee, he heard that old familiar "ding" coming from his computer announcing he had a message. Usually he didn't answer his e-mails until work started, but the sender caught his eye. "Interesting," he muttered. "I wonder who 'Emmy' is—and why is she writing to me this early?" He put down his coffee and opened the e-mail. It was addressed to him, but he could not read it. It was almost … cryptic. He remembered that Tony, down in the cafeteria, was into the "I Spy" thing and might enjoy doing a little homework. He hit print and then locked his workstation. He mentioned he was going down to the lunchroom to get a … donut. He tried to make it sound convincing when he asked if anyone else wanted one, but a few of his coworkers just smiled and a couple even said no thanks. As he was leaving, he grabbed the copy from the printer and was on his way.

On the way down the hallway, he kept trying to remember if he even knew an Emmy. He reached the cafeteria before he knew it and almost walked right past it. He walked in and almost all the lights were off. He thought how strange that was, given it opened at six every morning, and here it was almost eight. From across the room, he saw something under one of the lights that were on. It looked like a … a … body!

He ran over and saw it was his friend Tony. Bobby heard something banging into a table. He looked up in time to see someone running out the door. He didn't see who it was, but as the figure was leaving, on the back side of the hand that was holding the door open, Bobby saw a tattoo just above the knuckles. The tattoo looked like a palm tree.

Bobby looked back at Tony and noticed he had been stabbed—with a fork?

He looked closely at the fork and saw the design on it. It was a peace sign. *That looks familiar. Where have I seen that before?* Bobby wondered. He reached slowly for the fork. His breath was slow, his ears strained for a sound; time seemed to slow down.

Just before he touched the fork, in a faint and soft voice, he heard, "Help me … help me, please."

Bobby thought how strange and odd it sounded, and a feeling of nervousness surrounded him like a wet blanket. He looked all around to see if anyone was playing a joke on him, but no one else was there.

Then he heard the voice again: "Heelllpppp meeeeee, pleeeeeeassssse …" in a whisper that would send chills down the bravest of necks.

Bobby froze. He tried to move, but it was like a dozen strong men had a hold of him. Then, from the corner of his eye, he saw something. At first he thought it was a fly in the distance, moving back and forth. But as it got closer, it took on a form, a form that he remembered from his childhood, a form that would haunt him all his life. He tried to move, to yell, but the forces that held him would not let him go. The form moved closer, and he started to sweat. His body trembled. He felt the heat of the form as it moved closer still. The form was so close it cast a shadow over him now. He fought to move, but the invisible force field only tightened with each struggle to free himself.

Finally the form stopped and hovered over him, not touching, not moving, not making a sound. Bobby strained with all his might to look up, but it was like he was wearing a hat that weighed two hundred pounds. He moved ever so slowly. Then, as the form stood over him and he tried to look up, he could almost see it. A single drop of sweat moved into the corner of his right eye. He squeezed his eyes closed and winced at the pain for just a moment. In spite of the pain, in spite of the fear, despite the childhood memory, his thoughts, his worries, he forced his eyes open and saw, *and saw …*

*

Twenty-five years earlier, a little boy sits in his room playing with the Lincoln Logs he got the Christmas before. It's a beautiful summer day; the windows are open, and a breeze drifts in, bringing the smell of fresh summer flowers. Outside the window the small wind chimes softly clang against themselves and the birds sing their happy songs as the trees dance slowly side to side. In the backyard the family dog, Spike, pulls on his restraining chain to its full length and barks, as he wants to play with a squirrel just out of his reach.

Downstairs, his mom is preparing an evening meal. The smell of fresh green bell pepper and onions frying slowly winds its way through the house. She is listening to a radio station that is playing easy-listening music. She hums with each note that seems to dance up and down the hallway like an old movie. All is calm. You could not ask for a better day.

As the little boy plays with his toys with all his concentration, he does not hear the closet door slowly creak open. He does not notice the shadow that drifts back and forth like a fly off in the distance. He does not notice the shadow that drifts toward him in a slow and quiet way. Suddenly, the breeze stops blowing, and he can no longer hear the music playing or the birds singing. All is quiet. A chill runs down his spine like a glass of ice cold water being poured down his back. His mouth goes dry and he hears ...

"Hheeelllllloooooo, Bobby."

He freezes. There is only one voice, only one person who can make him feel this way. He slowly turns around and looks up and says, "Hello, Little Maggie. W-w-w-what brings you by so early?"

Little Maggie. The girl from down the street and over the railroad tracks. Little Maggie. Named after her mother, whom the whole town knew because she was always into everyone else's business. Little Maggie. Who would no doubt grow up to be just like her mom someday. Little Maggie. The new terror of this little, quiet town. Bobby did not like her because if she did not like the way things were going, she caused trouble and blamed someone else. Unfortunately, Bobby was the only other kid in the neighborhood who was close to her age. And what was worse, Bobby's mom liked her. She thought Little Maggie was an angel sent from above. Bobby also thought she was an angel—but not sent from *above*.

About three or four times a week, Little Maggie would come over to "play" with Bobby. If Bobby saw her coming he would hide, and Little Maggie would just go home. But today ... today Little Maggie did the hiding, and Bobby is cornered.

"Let's play house, Bobby," she says in a sweet little voice as she looks down at her new shoes. It seemed like she got a new pair at least once a week.

"Not today. I'm playing with my Lincoln Logs," he says, looking back down at his toys.

"Are you sure you don't want to play house, Bobby?" she asks a little slower as a grin stretches across her face.

Bobby starts getting that old feeling, like something is about to happen, something bad, something *very* bad. "Yyyyeess, I'm sure," he says slowly, looking over his shoulder toward her.

"Okay. If you don't want to play, I guess I'll have to do something … else."

Bobby's heart pounds, his throat dries up, and every pore in his body opens at once to let a flood of sweat pour out. He turns in fright to tell her he's changed his mind … but it's too late.

Little Maggie, sweet Little Maggie, is already running for the door, screaming at the top of her lungs, *"Don't touch me!"* At the same time she grabs her left blouse sleeve and pulls with all her might, ripping it as she runs out of the room.

Bobby loses his breath, his voice, and then his consciousness.

*

When he comes to, he slowly opens his eyes. At first, he only sees his mother fanning him with an old Japanese fan that Uncle Charles gave her when he was stationed in Japan with the US Navy. A feeling of calm washes across him like a wave on a beach. It was only a dream, only a dream. Then, off in a distance, he thinks he hears … something. At first he isn't quite sure what it is. Then he listens a little more. It sounds like, like … whimpering. *Oh, no, it can't be.* It couldn't be. Can it?

"Little Maggie, are you sure you're all right, honey?" he hears someone ask. Then, like turning on a light switch, that old feeling comes upon him in a flash. He slowly looks up and sees Little Maggie in the arms of her mother standing next to … a police officer. *A police officer?*

To this poor young boy, the room felt like it was spinning out of control, he dropped his head like a lead weight, and the room had gone black once more.

*

"Little Maggie? Is that you?" he said, finally able to move. He looked up from his kneeling position on the cafeteria floor. "Man, it's been a long, long time. What brings you here to my neck of the woods?"

"Little Maggie. Wow, I haven't heard that name in years. It's nice to be remembered, isn't it, Bobby?" she asked in a voice that was cold as ice.

Bobby shook out of his dream state and slowly got up off his knees as the feeling of being held slowly dissipated. He hadn't seen Little Maggie in more than twenty-five years. Although she was physically twenty-five years older, she somehow still looked like that same little terror of the neighborhood that he remembered. Bobby, who was now taller by five inches, looked down and said, "So, why *are* you here? How did you find me?"

"I still keep in touch with your mom," she said with a half smile, slightly looking up at him.

She keeps in touch with my mom? he thought. "Mom never said anything to me."

Maggie continued as if she didn't hear what he just said. "I've known where you've been ever since you left home."

"Okay, what do you want? Why now?"

Little Maggie slowly turned to face him, her hands clasped behind her, still looking down and drawing circles with her right toe. She said in a soft, gentle voice, "I … I need your help, Bobby."

That old feeling came drifting back, and Bobby thought he was going to pass out. He looked down and almost forgot about the body on the floor. He looked back at her, and then at the body, and shaking his head, he said in a barely audible voice, "What do you need, Little Maggie?"

"I've been looking for someone. Someone who has … certain … shall we say … information? He has a tattoo of a palm tree on the back of his hand. He got it a few years ago when he was in Jamaica."

Bobby hoped she didn't see his uneasiness as he remembered the shadow that ran out the cafeteria door a little while earlier.

"Who was this?" she asked as she looked down at the body.

"He was a friend of mine who worked here. I was just going to call the cops when …" His voice trailed off when he heard the double doors open.

It was a man in a suit, wearing a London Fog raincoat and a fedora, the police trailing behind him. The man in the suit walked up to Bobby and said, "Are you the guy who called this in? I'm Detective Steel. Can you tell me what happened?"

"We were just going to call you, Detective ..." Bobby started to say when the detective cut in.

"We?"

"Yeah, me and ..." Bobby turned to introduce Little Maggie, but she was gone.

"Who?" the detective pressed.

Bobby did not like to be pressed and finished by saying, "Yeah—me, myself, and I. Do you see anyone else here?"

The detective pointed his finger at Bobby and opened his mouth to say something, when one of the police officers said, "Hey, Detective. Check this out."

The detective closed his mouth, still looking at Bobby, and then said, "What is it?"

"It's a fork ... in his chest!" the officer said with a little distaste.

Finally the detective looked away from Bobby and said, "What?"

As the detective walked over to the body to examine it, Bobby looked around quickly to see where Little Maggie disappeared to but did not see her.

"Come on, get out of the way. Go do ... crowd control or something," Steel bellowed. He tilted his hat back on his head and looked at the fork and the design and said in a low voice, "I've seen this somewhere before."

He turned and yelled at Bobby, "So, are you going to tell me what happened, or do I need to drag you downtown and book you on suspicion of *murder*?"

"*Murder?*" Bobby yelled. "I wasn't even in here when it happened. Look, I came down here to ask Tony—"

Detective Steel cut him off. "Tony? Is that his name? What's his last name? Do you know where he lives? Is he married? How long has he worked here? How long have you known him?"

"Yes, Tony … is … his … name." Suddenly the thought of his friend lying there made the room spin. The gravity of the situation and the body on the floor in front of him now hit Bobby, and the lights grew dim. The last thing he heard was, "Someone catch him!"

Lights out.

CHAPTER 2

"It's raining, it's pouring, the old man is snoring ..." A song from the past played over and over in his head.

"Bobby, B-o-b-b-b-b-y. Are you awake?"

"Little Maggie? Is that you?" He opened his eyes and saw her standing there over him like something from a ... a memory.

"I'm sorry I had to disappear like that, but that's part of the story I started to tell you about, and I really don't need the police questioning me just yet. I really do need your help."

"Where am I?" Bobby asked, still half-asleep.

"You're in the hallway ... in the hospital. I followed you here. Look, you really need to help me find this guy. He has information that ... well ... that we *both* need."

"What are you talking about?" Bobby asked. His head felt a little clearer, and he lifted it off the pillow.

"You have to ... oh, no. Just relax and pretend I'm ... I don't know, I'm checking your chart or something."

That's when Bobby noticed she was wearing a nurse's uniform. "Okay," he said, putting his head back down on the bed.

"Someone will be right with you," Maggie said in a louder voice while turning away from the oncoming voices from the end of the hall. She walked away in the opposite direction.

"He's over there, Detective Steel," came the echo in the hall.

"Oh no, not him again," Bobby muttered.

"Oh, good, you're awake," Steel said in a chipper voice. "Now, where were we?"

"In the cafeteria," Bobby said slowly, his hand covering his eyes to shield the bright lights of the hallway.

Steel changed his demeanor. "Look, we can do this the hard way or the easy way. It's up to you."

The way he said it, it sounded like some TV show from the 1970s that you would watch at two in the morning. Bobby looked straight at him and repeated, "The hard way or the easy way? Come on, Detective, get out of the past, will ya?"

Detective Steel built up a full head of steam and was about to blow when a nurse appeared in the hallway. She approached them and said in a very nice voice, "Excuse me, gentlemen. I have to take the young man's vitals."

Like air being let out of a balloon, Steel deflated, and said in an easygoing voice, "We can continue this later, son."

Son? Who is he talking to? Bobby wanted to say out loud, but decided to just let it slide. As Steel walked away, the theme song to *Dragnet* popped into Bobby's head.

"Are you ready?" the nurse asked, still in her sweet voice.

"Ready when you are," Bobby replied.

She unlocked the wheels to his gurney and rolled him down the hall to an empty room filled with a lot of equipment. "I'll leave the lights off so they won't blind you. I'll be right back," she said, almost in a song.

Bobby started to relax and then began to think about the day's events. He thought about sitting at his desk in his cubical and getting that strange message on his computer. He thought about his friend, Tony, lying dead on the floor—and even stranger, Little Maggie showing up after all this time. Maybe it wasn't the fact that she just seemed to drop in but that she had known where he'd been and what he'd been doing for the past twenty-five years. And why did she choose to show up now? Why now? Something else bothered him, but he couldn't quite put his finger on it. There was something about ... about when they were kids. Something happened that he struggled to remember. Something about ...

"Hi, buddy. How are you doing?" came that voice from his past.

Bobby came out of his thoughts with a jump.

"Easy, Cowboy, I'm sorry to startle you. I was waiting for things to clear up a little before I tried to talk to you again," Maggie said in almost a whisper.

After Bobby started to breathe normally again, she continued. "So, will you help me? I don't have much time, and I have to talk to him ... before ..." She looked down at the floor and her voice trailed off.

"Before what, Little Maggie?" Bobby said a little impatiently.

"I can't really tell you anything more than that right now." She looked back up at him. "But I will tell you, you have to ..." She paused. "I hear the nurse coming. I'll stand over there in the corner, maybe she won't see me." Then she disappeared into a dark corner.

"You know I really hate it when you do that."

"Do what, Mr. Smith?" the nurse asked in a happy voice.

"Oh, umm … when you … ahh … pop right in. I didn't even hear you coming down the hallway. You're very light on your feet … like an … an angel."

"Why, thank you, Mr. Smith. I'll try to make more noise the next time. I mean, as much noise as an 'angel' will allow."

They both laughed as the she took his vitals.

The doctor came in after the nurse had finished and told him he was fine, nothing a good night's rest wouldn't take care of.

"You can leave whenever you're ready. Have a nice evening, Mr. Smith," the doctor said as he tapped the clipboard with his pen.

As the nurse walked out behind him, she looked back over her shoulder and smiled at Bobby, winked, and walked out the door.

"Have a nice evening, Mr. Smith. Boo-boo be do," came a childlike voice from the dark corner.

"Oh, stop it, Maggie. What are you, ten again?"

"Look," Maggie said, "I have to find out something on the next floor up. You go home, and I'll catch up with you later."

"Whatever," Bobby said, looking down at the floor as he slid off the gurney. "You just be careful. I don't want to have to bail you out of jail tonight for a break-in or anything."

Maggie was at the door, looking down the hallway. She turned halfway and said with a southern accent, "Why, Bobby Smith, I didn't know you still cared."

"Go on, and don't get caught," he said with a smile as she disappeared around the corner.

Bobby was released about fifteen minutes later after he signed some papers, and then he walked out the front door. He stood at the top of the stairs to the hospital and looked at his watch. Ten p.m. *Where did the day go?* he thought. He turned up his collar and looked at the cloudy sky as it started to sprinkle.

As he started down the stairs, he was so lost in thought that he didn't notice the dog sitting under some stairs on the street corner, chewing on a bone it had found near a trash can. He didn't notice the breeze that was starting to pick up, moving the leaves on the trees that lined the parking lot. He didn't notice the thunder or the lightning of the oncoming storm in the distance. He didn't notice the man across the street in an empty apartment stairwell, smoking a cigarette in the dark ... watching him leave.

And he didn't notice the smoker's hand on the railing ... the hand with a tattoo of a palm tree.

CHAPTER 3

Bobby got home, still lost in his own little world, trying to sort things out. He shook the rain off his jacket on the porch and took the key out of his pocket to unlock the door. He heard heavy footsteps behind him. Everything slowed down and it seemed to take longer than normal to turn around. His heart pounded—he heard the movement of his shirt and the heavy beating of the person's footsteps as they ran up behind him.

It all grew louder and louder when all of a sudden, in the flash of light from the sky, Bobby was hit from the side by this human freight train. He was hit with such a force that his feet left the floor for a good two yards, slamming the door into the wall. They flew past the entryway table. They were on their way past the living room doorway when they started to descend. Then, finally, they landed with a thud that might have been heard three blocks away and slid another six feet.

When Bobby stopped, with the little air in his lungs he could muster, he was trying to ask what was going on. All he got out was, "What the …" when his assailant, who had rolled with the fall, caught his balance and grabbed Bobby by his collar and started to drag him into the kitchen at the end of the hallway.

Bobby tried to catch his balance, and then he tried to yell, but nothing was going his way. All he managed was a few grunts as his assailant slammed him back and forth, from wall to wall in the hallway. They entered the kitchen. The assailant took two more steps and swung Bobby across the floor, slamming him against the lower cabinets. Bobby hit his back so hard that he lost the rest of his breath for a moment. As the thunder rolled outside, the assailant, a man who towered over Bobby, talked as if all was right with the world.

"Okay, now that I have your attention, I will ask the questions, and you will answer them. All right?"

Bobby tried to look up at him, but the stranger was standing between him and the kitchen light, so all Bobby saw was the dark outline.

The stranger took a step back and then two forward and kicked Bobby right in the stomach. "*All right?*" he yelled.

"Yeah, yeah, whatever you say," Bobby grunted with the little breath he had left.

"Good. Now where's the e-mail?" he asked in a very calm voice.

"E-mail?" Bobby said, recovering from the blow.

The stranger quickly knelt down and grabbed Bobby by the front of his shirt. Bobby felt him breathing on him; the smell of cigarettes was strong. Bobby slowly looked down and saw a tattoo on the back of his hand. A tattoo of a palm tree.

Bobby suddenly got cold, his face went pale, and it was as if every pore in his body opened up and sweat just poured out. Bobby started to get real dizzy, and then he was out cold.

Darkness, cold hard darkness. Shadows moving in and out. Sounds. Sounds of terror, sounds of pleading, and sounds of screaming. Then ... silence.

*

Where am I? Bobby thought. Slowly opening his eyes, he saw a bright light. It was the overhead light in the kitchen. He listened but didn't hear anything but the hum of the phone off the hook. With his head still spinning, he reached for something to steady himself while he attempted to maneuver himself up. He managed to grab hold of the corner of the kitchen table, adjusted his feet, and started to stand when all of a sudden—bang!—right back to the floor. His feet slipped right out from under him.

"Why is the floor wet?" he asked no one in particular. He slowly turned on his side to try and get up from all fours when he saw the floor. Bobby tried to scream but nothing came out. He tried to move faster but just slipped and slid. He could not move fast enough from the blood on the floor or the dead body next to him.

"Look who decided to join the land of the living. You know, you really should see a doctor about those blackouts," Little Maggie said as she wiped her blood-soaked hands with one of his dish towels.

Bobby spun around so fast that he slipped in the blood again and landed on his opposite side. "Who, why, what ... *what's going on?*"

"I think you mean to say, 'Who, *what*, and then *why*,'" Maggie said sarcastically.

"*Little Maggie*! Look at me!" he yelled as he finally got to his feet. "I'm covered in *blood*!"

"Well," she said sympathetically, "at least it isn't yours."

"What happened? Did you see any of it?"

"I don't think you really want to know what happened, Bobby," she said quietly.

"Maggie, if you know something, you'd better tell me *now!*"

"Don't talk to me like that, little man. Remember the last time you talked to me like that?" She said looking up at him, coldly.

Bobby stopped for a moment and thought about that. His thoughts took him back about twenty-eight years, when he was just eight and she was seven. Little Maggie had come over one day, as she usually did, and while his mom was working in the garden in the front yard, they were in the backyard.

"Want to play grown up?" Little Maggie asked as she watched him while he swung on the gym set his dad had bought a couple of years before.

"What's that?" Bobby asked.

"I will be the mommy, and you will be the daddy. You go to work and bring me all the money."

"That doesn't sound like fun."

"Well, I want to play, and you're gonna do what I want!" she said angrily.

"No I won't, Little Maggie. I'm never doing what you say again!" Bobby yelled as loud as he could.

"Oh no?" she asked in a sweet little voice.

"No!" he yelled, still swinging.

"Okay then," she said calmly. Little Maggie walked around behind him and picked up a branch that had fallen from a windstorm a couple of days earlier. She held it like a baseball bat as she walked back around in front of him. He made a backward swinging motion. She stopped in front and just to the right of his path forward. As he was on his way forward again, he started to yell, louder and louder until the makeshift bat connected with his face, knocking him clear off the swing, sending him backward to the ground.

Little Maggie had dropped the broken branch and simply walked home.

*

Back in the kitchen, Bobby stood there looking at the bloody mess in his kitchen and his clothes. His face, which had been wrinkled with frustration slowly smoothed out, and he was calmer once more. "Sorry, Maggie, I was just upset because I don't know what happened, that's all," he said in an almost childlike voice.

"Hey, it's water under the bridge," she said. "You'd better get this place cleaned up before someone comes over, like that detective friend of yours." She turned, tossed the towel into the sink, and started to walk out.

"*Little Maggie!*" Bobby yelled.

Maggie stopped and slowly turned halfway around. "How quickly we forget," she said slowly and as cold as ice.

Bobby froze. He took a deep breath, and slowly, and a lot more calmly, he said, "I mean, *Maggie*. What happened here?"

"Sleep on it, Bobby, dear. You'll remember. You'll remember everything." And with that, she turned and walked out the door.

When there is a dead animal in the road, it affects people differently. Some cover their eyes and don't look.

Some are curious, so they slow down and try to figure out what kind of animal it was. Most of us have numbed ourselves to the sight of roadkill.

But a dead person is a whole other ball game. We are taught from birth that killing is wrong and that we would be caught and would be prosecuted and then sentenced to the fullest extent of the law, some to death and others to a life in prison. It's not like the movies. In the movies, the dead actor comes back in another show or series. But in real life, you can smell, feel, and touch the dead body. In real life, dead people don't come back to life, especially ones with a whole bunch of knife holes in them—like the one lying on Bobby's kitchen floor.

Bobby's stomach spun. He would have thrown up, but he couldn't remember the last time he'd eaten. The room was growing dark; he fought the feeling of passing out with all his might. And then he lost.

Every once in a while we sleep a deep, deep sleep. And in that deep sleep, it's been said, we can travel back in time and remember things we either chose to forget or simply don't remember. This was where Bobby had gone to now.

All was dark, but he heard the sound of children's feet on a hardwood floor. He heard them yelling and laughing. The echo of their voices sounded like they were coming from a really big room but moved somehow slower than in real life. The darkness gave way to light, and he saw the old house he grew up in. It was twenty-five years ago and he was a little boy again, about eleven, wearing shorts and a white polo shirt. He was running through the house with … Little Maggie. Little Maggie? He had to really think about it, but they did have a few days that they did have fun. This dream, this memory, was one such day. Little Maggie was dressed up, as usual, this time in a blue dress with white piping and, to match her dress, a blue ribbon in her long brunette hair.

"No running in the house, kids," his mom said from the kitchen as she was preparing lunch for them that rainy afternoon.

As they came running down the stairs, Bobby said, "Okay, we won't."

"*Bobby!*" she yelled as the sound of thunder boomed outside over the house. They both froze.

For a moment they were quiet, and then he said, "Yes?"

"I said no running in the house, all right?"

"Yes, Mom."

"Why don't you and Little Maggie come in here for lunch now?"

Bobby whispered, "I'll race you. Last one to the table has to eat the dog food!"

"Okay, *go!*" Little Maggie said and took two steps and tripped over the hallway rug. "Darn these new shoes," she complained.

"Ha-ha!" Bobby said as he ran to the kitchen.

"Bobby Smith, didn't I tell you *no running* in the house?"

"Yes, ma'am."

"Now take the silverware to the table and *no more running.*"

Bobby took the silverware and turned toward the table facing away from the kitchen doorway. He saw the lighting flash and heard the thunder. He heard the footsteps coming up behind him. He heard Little Maggie trip, and then he saw …

CHAPTER 4

B obby woke up in a fright. It was the next morning, and he was in his own bed with the alarm going off. He sat straight up, very confused. *What's going on?* he thought. He shut off the alarm and slowly pulled back the covers. He was in his shorts and T-shirt ... and he was clean.

"Where's all the ..." He jumped out of bed in a fit of panic and ran into the kitchen to finish with "blood?" The kitchen was clean. Everything had been put back into its own place. Now the important question. "Did this really happen or what?" he said.

"Oh, it really happened. Look at this morning's paper," came the voice behind him.

Like someone just stuck an electric cord in his pocket, Bobby jumped so high he thought he would hit the ceiling. "*Maggie!*" he screamed. When he calmed down and caught his breath, he said, "I really wish you'd stop doing that."

"Stop being such a baby. Here." She tossed the paper on the table.

The front-page headline read, "Man Murdered: Stabbed 32 Times."

As Bobby looked at the paper, he said, "What does this have to do with ..." He stopped. The picture of the body, which was covered with a sheet, only had one exposed part, the left hand. Bobby froze when he saw the tattoo of the palm tree on it. "I don't understand. How can this be?" Bobby asked slowly and quietly.

"You really need to relax. I told you to think about it, and you would remember, but you keep fighting it. Now go have some breakfast and go back to bed, because I really think you need to relax. Besides, it's Saturday, and you don't have anything planned, do you?"

"No, no I don't. How did you know?"

"You must have told me last night when we were cleaning up or something. I have some errands to run. I'll talk to you later." She started for the door.

"Hey, Little Maggie?" Bobby said quietly.

She stopped and did an about-face that would impress any military person.

"Thanks," he said, still looking at the paper.

She gave him a half smile and said, "Don't thank me yet. We still have some things to take care of." She did another about-face and walked away.

Bobby slowly looked up and started to get that old feeling again.

Within the next half hour, Bobby had eaten and cleaned up his breakfast, all the while thinking about what Little Maggie had said. Not so much about the "relax" thing or about the newspaper article, but about the night before. "You must have told me last night when *we* were cleaning up or something" is what she said. Cleaning up? *I helped her clean up?* he thought. He put the dish towel on the refrigerator's door handle, yawned and stretched and headed for the bedroom.

Closing the bedroom door, he heard it latch and thought how strange it was that he heard that noise and how it seemed to echo throughout the house. If the bedroom door would make that much noise, why hadn't he heard the front door make just as much noise when Maggie left? He staggered a couple of steps, grabbed his head, and fell toward the bed, hitting it in the middle.

*

"No running in the house, kids," said his mom from the kitchen as she was preparing lunch for the both of them, like an old forty-five broken record, skipping back.

They both came running down the stairs in slow motion, Bobby yelling, "Okay, we won't."

"*Bobby!*" she yelled as the sound of thunder boomed outside over the house.

He could see it all happening again and again.

"Yes?"

"I said *no* running in the house, all right?"

"Yes, Mom."

"Why don't you and Little Maggie come in here for lunch now?"

He leaned over to Maggie and whispered, "I'll race you, last one to the table has to eat the dog food"

"Okay, *go!*" Little Maggie said as she slowly turned and took the two steps and tripped over the hallway rug. After she hit the floor and rolled, he heard, "Darn new shoes."

"Ha-ha," Bobby said as he ran into the kitchen.

"Bobby Smith," his mother yelled as she spun in place to face him. "Didn't I tell you *no running* in the house?"

"Yes, ma'am," he said quietly.

"Now take the silverware to the table and *no more running.*"

Bobby took the silverware and started to turn toward the table facing away from the kitchen doorway. He saw the lighting flash and heard the thunder.

He has seen this scene many times and tries to stop it, but he can't. He hears the footsteps coming up behind him. He hears her trip, and then sees Little Maggie falling, falling toward him, falling toward the silverware.

CHAPTER 5

Across town, Detective Steel was working on a murder case: Tony from the lunchroom.

"No one deserves to die like this," he said, standing over the body at the morgue with a cup of coffee in his left hand, his right hand in his pocket, jingling some change. He was dressed in a blue two-piece pinstriped suit he picked up from Sears when he made detective about five years ago. He wore a gray fedora felt hat, cocked back on his head, like the private investigators did in the old black-and-white movies. He kept his hair short and his mustache trimmed, the same way he did when he was in the army, even thought he only did five years with the MPs and got out almost twenty-six years ago. He was in good shape; he ran three times a week and swam every Thursday afternoon about three miles, after his shift.

As he stood there, with his tie slightly loosened and top button unbuttoned, he talked to the coroner. "Have you ever seen anything like this before, Doc?" Steel asked, still looking at the body.

"Only in an accident, not in a murder."

"*Accidents?* That's it?" the detective yelled.

"What's the matter? Are you okay?" the coroner asked.

"Yeah, yeah. Let me see the murder weapon again," he said, snapping his fingers at the doctor.

"You mean 'the *fork*.' Why can't you guys watch something else other than old cop movies? All you guys are so dramatic," the coroner muttered as he went over to where the tray with the fork was still in its plastic bag.

"Okay then, the *fork*. May I see the *fork*, please?" Steel asked in a heavy voice, a little impatient.

"Sure thing, Detective. Here to scrve, here ... to ... serve," the doctor said in a lighthearted voice.

Steel snatched it from the coroner's hand, staring down at him the whole time. He paused for dramatic effect, but the coroner seemed unaffected. He smiled, turned, and walked back over the tray.

Steel studied the fork. "Where have I seen this, where have I ... I remember," he said softly. "I remember."

CHAPTER 6

B obby jumped out of bed and put on some blue jeans and a T-shirt that said "The Who, Live" on the front over a flag of England. But Bobby wasn't himself. He had a look of determination about him that seemed somehow … urgent. Everything he did seemed quick and abrasive. Even the tension in his face was much more than normal as he put on his sneakers. "Time to finish this once and for all," he said, a strange look in his eye. "Once … and … *for … all!*"

*

Back in town, Detective Steel walked into the police station and yelled, "Helen, I want you to pull a file for me. It's from about twenty or twenty-five years ago and had to do with some kid down on McKinney Street."

"I'll get to it right after lunch, boss."

"Now, Helen. Order in. I'll take the number three from what's-its-name around the corner," he said as he walked into his office putting his gun in his out file box.

Helen made the call to the local sandwich shop and then poked her head into the detective's office. "It's gonna be about thirty minutes because it's starting to rain."

"Good, that should give you just enough time to find that folder. I think it's in a cabinet in the dungeon."

"The dungeon?" she asked with a little trill in her voice.

"Yeah, yeah in the *basement*, the dungeon! What, did I stutter or something? Let's go, chop-chop."

Helen stood at the door for a moment longer to see if he would say he was just kidding. But he didn't. He looked up from his desk and flicked his wrist at her as if shooing a little child. She turned and walked slowly toward the basement door as the thunder started to roll in the distance.

The basement. Like some scary movies, the basement is where things happen, with a few windows, the dark corners, the dampness, and sounds that seem to come from nowhere. This particular basement had all that and then some. First of all, it was nicknamed "the dungeon" because when the police station opened about sixty years ago, the holding cells were in the basement. And like most places, someone stood up and complained that it was too damp, not enough lighting, and cold. A terrible place to put muggers, robbers, and thieves. So the state forked up the big bucks to build a nicer place, so they could be comfortable before they were sentence to a life in prison. Even though the cells were still there, the doors were taken off so no one could "accidentally" lock themselves in. It was now "the vault." You could trace any crime or disturbance that had ever been committed, or should I say recorded, in this little town. Like most old buildings around town, this one had stories of ghosts, murder, and death, and if you really listened, you could hear … something.

Helen slowly opened the creaking door to the basement, and the cool, musty breeze hit her like a light slap on the face. She cringed for just a moment and then opened the door a little more. As she did, she thought she heard a voice groan. She stopped and waited. She opened the door a little more. The groan intensified, and she stopped pushing the door again as the groaning stopped. One more push on the door ... and she realized it was just the hinges. A sigh of relief, and she pushed the door all the way open and stood there for a moment, looking at the dark stairs as a lightning bolt flashed outside, the sound of thunder getting closer.

The hair on the back of her neck stood straight up when she heard ...

"It would help if you turned on the lights," came a low voice from behind her.

Helen screamed so loud that everyone in the station came out from where they were to see what happened.

"Helen, Helen, calm down. It's only me," John, one of the patrolmen, said as he grabbed her arm to prevent her from falling down the stairs.

"*John!* Why you ... *never* do that again! I'm too young to have a heart attack."

"Sorry," John said sarcastically, as he turned to walk away. "I'll never try to help you again."

"What's going on out there?" Steel bellowed from his office doorway. "Helen, did you get me that file yet? I'm waiting."

"*I'm getting it!* I'm getting it," she said in a voice that trailed off as she turned back to the stairs and turned on the light. One more deep breath and down she went.

Forty years of ... stuff. That's what the dungeon had been reduced to. There was a small path that snaked back and forth around the room, ending at some file cabinets. Helen bumped her elbow on a chair leg that was sticking out a little too far as she was stepping over one of the five dehumidifiers in the room.

"Ouch!" she yelped. Her voice echoed and bounced around the room until it didn't sound like her voice anymore. "Is someone there?" she asked slowly. No answer. Looking around, she continued her trek. When she reached the file cabinets, she used her finger to point to the dates on the outside of the drawers as she talked to herself. "Let's see … 1970 to '75, '75 to '80 … here we go," and as if timed just right, lighting flashed. "And 1980 to '85." She heard a noise behind her, and the sound of thunder, but she refused to let her imagination run away with herself. "Let's see, McKinney Street." Another noise, a little closer. "I'm not going to turn around," she said to calm herself.

"Okay," a voice behind her said.

Every nerve in her body broke at the same time. Helen let out a scream that would have woken the dead. She had a death grip on the file as her arms and legs went in every which direction. When she finally stopped, after what seemed like ten minutes, she turned and saw—

"Are you finished with your little dancing act, Helen? Holy moly!" Detective Steel yelled. "Did you find the file yet?"

Helen did a 180 with her feelings. She went from totally scared to being … well … totally scary. "Why you … you … big … pain in my neck! *Here!*" With a force of ten men, Helen slammed the file into the detective's chest and pushed past him. In her haste, as she stepped over the dehumidifier again, she bumped her other arm into the same chair leg that was still sticking out into the aisle. She grabbed her arm and turned to the chair and yelled at it, "And you're *next!*" She made her way through the rest of the basement without incident, stamped her way up the stairs, and slammed the door closed.

Steel, still standing there with his mouth partway opened, snapped it shut and blinked as the door slammed. "Oh, by the way, your lunch is here," he said quietly as he turned his attention back to the file.

Steel grabbed a chair from a pile and sat down. The storm had moved overhead and was getting louder and the rain heavier. He opened the file and started to go through it. "Robbery ... robbery ... break-in ... hijacking ... ah, here it is. Accidental death."

A bolt of lightning flashed with a crack of thunder that almost shook the place. Just then the lights went out. A small window on the street side of the building was the only source of light. He squinted in the little light to read the file.

"I would have made it," came a very soft voice from one of the cells.

"Who said that?" Steel yelled as he jumped up from his chair and reached for the gun that was not there.

"I could have made it if it weren't for you, Steel." The voice was almost a whisper and seemed to move around the room.

Steel snapped his head around to see if he could see someone, anyone. "What are you talking about?" The rain was coming down in buckets. From a dark corner of the cell, a shadow emerged and slowly moved toward Steel.

Steel stuttered when he said, "W-w-who are you? What do you w-w-want from me?"

"You could have saved me. You could have done something. It's all your fault that I am ... dead!"

Steel had not been this scared for many years. He thought about that for just a fraction of a second.

"You do remember, don't you? That's why you came down here for the file."

"That wasn't my fault. I did what I could. I did what I was supposed to! *It was a very long time ago!*" he yelled.

"You could have saved me, and now you must pay!"

Steel turned and tried to run through the dark basement. He took two or three big steps toward the door and tripped over the dehumidifier. As he fell, he grabbed at anything and everything to catch his fall. A flash of lightning lit up the room for just a moment, and he saw a hand dart out with a fork pointing up. He tried to yell, but it was too late. The fork pierced the detective's chest, and dark blood poured out of the holes in his chest. He rolled over onto his back, gasping for air.

A voice moved in close to his ear and said, "Let's see how long it takes *you* to die." The sound of thunder rolled across the sky.

Steel's breathing grew shorter and shorter. He flashed back to the scene of an accident twenty-five years ago. There was a young girl lying on a kitchen floor with a sheet covering her body; it was a rainy afternoon. The thunder cracked overhead. Young Patrolman Steel was the first officer on the scene. This was the first real investigation of his career, and he needed to impress his seniors. He wiped off the rain from his coat as he walked though the house, taking statements from everyone there, and he did everything he was taught—except one thing.

The young patrolmen didn't do the most important thing first: *check the body*. He didn't ask where the sheet came from, the sheet Bobby's mother had put over Little Maggie to relieve the sight of what they thought was a dead body in her kitchen. He didn't notice the movement of the sheet as Little Maggie lay there on the floor, short on breath and unconscious.

He radioed in the report and told the dispatcher to have the ambulance take its time because "the body isn't going anywhere." He didn't find out that she could have made it until the ambulance arrived, and as they put her on a gurney, the two attendees heard her moan one last time.

The attendees pulled Steel off to the side and told him they had just heard her moan. Steel grabbed them by the collars, fearing his seniors would find out he had made a mistake on a scene where someone died, and forced them up against the side of the ambulance. He threatened them that if they ever mentioned that again, they would pay with their lives.

By the time they got to the hospital, Little Maggie was pronounced dead from a stab wound to the chest. It was ruled an accident and no charges were brought forth.

About fifteen years later, just after Sergeant Steel got his gold shield and became Detective Steel, he heard from one of the ambulance attendants. He claimed he had some information about a certain crime scene that might "accidentally surface" unless the attendant receive some compensation. Steel, not wanting this to get out, not after making detective and all, paid to keep his mouth shut. The attendant promised he was going to disappear to some island in the Caribbean. He returned only a couple of months ago from Jamaica with a tattoo on his left hand to try to get more money from Steel written in an email that was coded. And what happened to the other attendant? He tried to make an honest living in the food service industry. Until recently, he worked in a small kitchen in a cafeteria in a government building off 95. He found out what his old partner was up to and was going to blow the whole thing wide open when the guy with the tattoo, shall we say, changed his mind.

"Ah, you do remember, don't you?" came the whisper from his left ear.

"Who … who are you?" came the detective's gurgled voice.

"Who am I? Why, Detective, I'm crushed you don't remember. Here, let me show you …" The shadow moved in so Steel could get a look at his killer.

"You're that guy from the cafeteria … Bobby … Bobby something." Steel strained to focus.

Steel heard an almost possessed voice. "Look again."

In between the lighting flash and the thunder crack, Bobby's face changed to Little Maggie's. A young girl with perfect skin, long brunette hair flowing over her shoulders with a blue ribbon tied on top, a bright smile, and blue eyes that were as cold as ice. In a sweet young voice she said, "You could have saved me, Detective. You could have saved me."

"I was young. It was my first investigation. I made a mistake. It's been twenty-five years, for Pete's sake."

"It has been twenty-five years. Twenty-five years … *today*! Now say good-bye, Detective Steel."

With the next lighting flash and the last crack of thunder, Little Maggie pushed the fork deeper into his chest. Detective Steel let out one last breath and died. The shadow sprinkled some silverware around the floor, dropped the box next to his head, and disappeared into the dark.

The rain started to let up and the lighting flashes were lessening. Only a few rumbles in the distant sky were all that was left of the present storm. There was movement once again on the street—cars splashing in the puddles, people putting away their umbrellas, the sky starting to clear to give way to the light of day. No one noticed the downed branches from the wind. No one noticed the river in the streets starting to slow and then disappear. No one noticed that the rain had now stopped, and no one noticed the shadow of a man walking out of a basement door from the side of the police station, a door that hadn't been used in many years.

No one noticed.

CHAPTER 7

Bobby woke in his bed, and for the first time in a long time he felt well rested. He got up and jumped into the shower and even sang a song with a catchy jingle. He went to the kitchen and made coffee. As he filled a cup, he heard a knock on the back kitchen door.

He yelled, "Come on in!" Then he thought that was strange because first of all, no one ever came to the back door and secondly, he never remembered unlocking it, *ever*.

But the door opened and he said, "I was wondering when you were gonna come back. You were right. A good night's sleep, and I feel so much better. Would you like a cup of coffee, Little Maggie?"

"No, thanks. You see, you should listen to me more often," she said.

"I'm still a little confused though, about where you've been all these years," Bobby said as he sat at the dining room table.

"I told you, all you have to do is relax and you would remember. Now," she said as she walked up behind him and started to run her fingers through his hair, "relax and remember … relax and remember …" Her voice seemed to drift off as Bobby started to fall asleep.

*

"No running in the house, kids," he heard his mom say from the kitchen

He heard the thunder and the rain once more.

They were running down the stairs, as he was answering, "Okay, we won't."

"*Bobby!*" he heard her say as the sound of thunder rolled outside over the house.

"Yes?"

"I said *no* running in the house, all right?"

"Yes, Mom."

"Why don't you and Little Maggie come in here for lunch now?"

He whispered, "I'll race you, last one to the table has to eat the dog food!"

Little Maggie said, "Okay, *go!*"

Then he heard her take two steps and trip over the hallway rug. "Darn new shoes."

He felt the soft breeze on his face as he ran into the kitchen. "Ha-ha!"

"Bobby Smith, didn't I tell you *no running* in the house?"

"Yes, ma'am."

"Now take the silverware to the table and *no more running.*"

He can see himself taking the silverware, the silverware with the peace sign on the handle that his dad has had since he was a teenager, and he sees himself starting to turn toward the table facing away from the kitchen doorway. He can see the lightning flash, he can hear the thunder. He can hear the footsteps coming up behind him in an echoing sound. That's when he heard poor Little Maggie trip … and she fell onto the forks he was carrying. As she fell on top of him, he tried to move the forks out of the way, but they got stuck on her dress. They both hit the floor with a thud.

His mom turned around to see them both on the floor and she started to laugh, not knowing what happened. She walked over to the refrigerator and grabbed the towel off the handle and said in a cheery voice, "Okay, you two, let's not stay on the floor all afternoon."

It wasn't until Little Maggie started to wheeze that Bobby's mom realized there was something a little more wrong than what she originally thought.

"Bobby? What happened? Help me … please!" Little Maggie said in more breath than speech.

Bobby froze. He could not say anything but, "I'm sorry, Little Maggie, I'm sorry."

Bobby's mom rushed over and picked up Little Maggie, who gave a loud inhale, and laid her flat on her back.

"I'm sorry, Little Maggie, I am so sorry," Bobby kept repeating. He went to pull the fork out of the little girl's chest, but his mom stopped him and explained that it might do more damage than good. Then his mom went into the living room to call for help.

Bobby carefully picked up Little Maggie's head and rested it on his legs as he sat down beside her. Running his fingers through her long brunette hair, he tried to comfort her. "I'm sorry, Little Maggie, I didn't mean for you to get hurt. Mom's calling for some help right now. You're gonna be all right. Please be all right. I'm sorry."

In a faint voice, Little Maggie said, "It's all right, Bobby. I know you didn't mean it. It's just these darn"—she winced in pain—"shoessssss," she finished.

"Little Maggie? *Little Maggie?*" Bobby yelled.

His mom dropped the phone and ran back into the kitchen and over to them.

Bobby said, "I think she's stopped breathing, Mom. What do I do? *What do I do?*"

His mom tried to listen for her breath but didn't hear anything. In a very quiet voice, she said, "She's gone, sweetie. Little Maggie is gone."

Bobby slowly lifted the little girl's head once more and slid out from under her, lowering her head back to the floor very easy. He slowly walked over to the kitchen table and sat down, staring at the body of his friend, which now lay lifeless on the floor. No tears, no sobbing, not a sound did he make. He simply locked it up inside himself and stared at her on the floor.

His mother went into the other room for just a moment and returned with a sheet and covered the body. Just after she covered the body, they heard the oncoming sirens of the police. Bobby did not move.

The young officer shook off the rain, walked through the house, asked a lot of questions, and then left. Bobby watched as they wheeled Little Maggie out the door, and he turned away just as a small commotion started outside with the officer and the ambulance drivers, and then Bobby walked upstairs to his room. He sat on the edge of his bed and watched the rain through the window.

His mom looked in on him and asked if he was okay.

Bobby answered, "Yeah, I think so. I'm just going to watch the weather cry for a little while." Then he dropped his head and whispered, "Someday, Little Maggie, I'll make this up to you. Someday."

*

The little boy turned into a man sitting by himself at a dining room table, his head hanging. "I'm sorry, Little Maggie. I didn't know," he said softly. And then like the breaking of a damn, everything came back to him from all his blackouts like a flood of memories. The cafeteria, that awful night in the kitchen and the afternoon in the dungeon. It all came back.

CHAPTER 8

A few months later, across town, the sun was shining, and a car pulled up to an almost-empty parking lot. The car door opened and the driver got out, taking off his sunglasses and slipping them into his pocket as he walked across a gravel lot. He carried a bouquet of flowers. He walked through some trees and well-cut grass. He walked down a path that many people have traveled for many years. He looked up and felt the sunshine on his face as he breathed in the fresh air. All was quiet, all was still. He noticed off to his left some people embracing each other who seemed to be crying. He turned his attention forward again and walked a little farther up the path, making a right turn to the seventh headstone.

"Hey, Little Maggie. How are you doing?" Bobby knelt on one knee and brushed leaves off the site, placing the flowers in a vase attached to the headstone, which read

Maggie Emmy Preston
Who was taken much too early in life. She will be missed.
1974–1984

"I'm sorry I haven't been by lately, kinda busy and all. But things are quieting down, we got a new detective and he seems all right. The papers reported that Detective Steel's death was an accident. They said it was just a matter of time before someone got hurt in the basement of the police station because of the way things are kept down there. They said he tripped over some stuff, some evidence of some accident from the 1980s, or something. What a terrible way to go. They still haven't caught the person who killed Tony. Maybe they never will. Nobody ever found out how that other guy died either. The last thing anyone heard was that he was some drifter from Jamaica or somewhere who was in the wrong place at the wrong time. Anyway, I just thought I would stop by and say hi. I haven't had any blackouts in a couple of months now. I knew they would go away … you just have to be patient and just relax about these things, that's all. 'Things will work out in the end,' Mom always says. I'll tell her you said hi. Take care, and I'll stop by again soon."

He stood up and brushed the grass from his pant leg. He started to walk away and then stopped, turned around, and walked back over, kneeling again, placing his hand on the headstone. In a low, somber voice, he said, "I really am sorry, Maggie. I didn't mean to hurt you. I'm really sorry." He stood up, wiped his eyes, and walked away.

He was almost to his car when he felt a breeze blow by him, and for a moment he thought he heard a little girl's voice say, "It's all right, Bobby, I know."

Bobby looked back and smiled, put on his sunglasses, got back into his car, and drove away.

EPILOGUE

....

Back in the editor's office, Robert closed the file and went to light another cigarette, but the pack was empty. He noticed the coffee was all gone too. It was late afternoon, and he decided the lunch crowd would be long gone by now. The dinner crowd would not have started yet, so he thought he would go to the diner for some fresh coffee, some fresh air, and some fresh conversation with the writer.

When he got down to the sidewalk, the day's heat was tapering off. It was starting to get a little humid, like any day in the early summer. He was about a block away from the diner when Sean walked out of another store in front of him.

"Just the guy I was looking for," Robert said.

Sean looked up with a little shock.

"Do you have a little time for something to drink over at the diner?" Robert asked in a cheery voice.

"Yeah, I guess so," Sean said in a voice that sounded like he was just called to the head office.

They walked that last block without talking, which made Sean a little nervous. They walked into an almost empty diner, and Robert told Sean to grab a table while he got the drinks. Sean found one in the back next to the big picture window that overlooked the intersection and busy sidewalk, away from everyone else.

Robert came over with a tall cup of coffee and a tall glass of root beer for Sean. Sean took it with a smile and grabbed a straw from the holder as Robert sat down. As Sean was taking the paper off the straw and not looking up, he asked, "Well, what did you think?"

"Besides a few spelling mistakes, I liked it. I mean I really liked it. It was much better than your last … I don't know, dozen stories, I guess. What's the change?"

Sean took a moment to look out the window, through the people on the sidewalk, over the cars in the intersection, over the trees in the park across the way, and into the darkening sky of a possible late-day shower. Then, after a deep breath, he looked at Robert and asked in a low voice, "How long have I been here in this town? Three? Four years now? You and Sara are really the first people I met, and that was the day after I drove in here. It was over at the supermarket in the frozen-foods section when I accidentally bumped into your cart. I said something off-handed like I just got into town, and I didn't know where I was going, or something like that. You smiled and made a joke to make me feel better. You invited me out to dinner, and we talked about the present and the future, but not about the past. Do you remember? And still, you have never asked."

"You looked down on your luck, and I didn't want to stir up things or make it sound like I was nosy," Robert said and then took a sip of his coffee. "Besides, I always thought that when you were ready, you would tell us."

Sean looked out the window again, but this time he wasn't looking at the weather, he was looking for the words. And without looking at Robert this time, he said, "In a way, I did tell you about my past. You've always said, 'Write about what you know,' and I did. The one thing I like about writing is …" He looked at Robert with misty eyes. "You can use any name you want."

Robert quickly put down his cup of coffee because he thought he was going to drop it. There was a long moment of silence, and then, in the distance, a short flash of lightning followed by the sound of thunder.

LIFE IN A FLASH

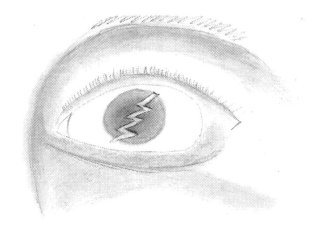

My name is William B. Stanley, and I am writing all this down at the request of my doctor, who thinks it will help me to remember things and events that have happened to me since the accident. *Accident*, my foot. I think the guy did it on purpose.

It all started what seems like a lifetime ago ... maybe? It was August 30, 2012, and I was the safety officer on the new construction site downtown. It started as a beautiful summer day with the sun shining and a warm breeze blowing from the west. I ran downstairs to be with the family for breakfast. A typical scene for us would be Amanda over the stove cooking eggs; Tommy, twelve, eating cereal; Brian, nine, finishing up his homework; and Joann, four, sitting at the table she could barely see over.

I walked into the kitchen putting my work bag on the floor next to the door and kissed Amanda on the cheek. I said, "Please, something quick, I have to finish a couple of reports before my meeting at ten."

Tommy said, "Dad? I think I know what college I want to go to."

"College? Can you wait until you finish high school first?"

"But Dad," Tommy protested, "the teacher said college is going to be the most important decision we will ever make in our lives."

"Does your teacher have any kids of her own?" I asked as I sat down with the paper.

"Ah … I don't think so," Tommy said, looking at the ceiling, tapping his spoon against his chin.

"You'll make a lot of important decisions in your life, Tommy. College will only be one of them. Finish high school—heck, finish middle school first—and then we'll talk. Okay?"

"All right," Tommy said, a little disappointed as he rested his head on one hand with his elbow on the table. In the other hand was a spoon, and he put it back in the bowl and made circles in his cereal.

"I'm going into the navy so I can see the world," Brian said enthusiastically, looking up from his book.

"You … I'd be happy if you would just finish your homework when you get home from school and not at the breakfast table."

"Okay," Brian said, looking back down at his book.

"I'm going to be a princess and live in a big castle," Joann said with a really big smile.

"Sweet pea, you can be anything you want to be." Then I paused a moment and looked over my paper at the boys but was still talking to her. "After you finish high school and after you finish college. Okay?" I said, straightening my paper to read it again.

"Okay," she said with a little enthusiasm. After a moment of silence, she added, "Can my husband go to the same college as me?"

I dropped my paper, Amanda dropped some silverware she was washing, Brian looked up from his book, and Tommy said, "What … what did she say?" We all looked at Joann for a moment.

Then she sat up straight to look over the table better and said a little louder, "I said …"

"That's okay," I broke in, "we all heard you the first time. Once was enough. We will have to wait and see if *he* can go or not, okay?"

"Okay," she said, satisfied with the answer.

I looked at Amanda and said, "Out of the mouths of babes. Boy, your daughter comes up with some real winners."

"*My* daughter?" she said, throwing some water at me. "I seem to remember that she is *your* daughter as well."

We all started laughing, and then I looked at my watch and jumped up and said, "I have to go."

I kissed Amanda and said, "I should be home regular time. Kids, study hard and—"

At the same time, all three kids said, "And be safe."

"Very good. Love you all, see you soon." I picked up my work bag and headed out the door.

It was late afternoon with the sun seeming to fall out of the sky and with time slipping away very fast. We were working on what was to be called the 'Downtown Medical Center, a Hospital for the People.' I could see it all now happening again in my mind as if it just happened. Bobby Dull (whom we called "Never Dull" because he was always doing something that would get attention. For instance, one day a couple of weeks ago, I noticed him hanging from an I beam over the end of the building. I found out later that he did it on a dare. I mean, really, are we still in elementary school where "I double dog dare you" takes priority over safety?). Anyway, I "grounded" him for a week. He had to stay on the ground floor to do cleanup work. I really don't think he liked that very much. Oh, not the cleaning up part, he could handle that, but the cut in pay part. I mean, did he really think we were going to pay journeyman's wages for cleaning up?

So after the week, he came back up the top floor to do his carpentry work again. Bobby is very good at what he does; it's just that sometimes he doesn't seem to act very ... responsible. Anyway, the day of the "accident," I was walking through the jobsite and then went up the stairwell. When I opened the door to the fourth floor where Bobby was working, I saw him plugging in a drill. Now since this is a union job, he, as a carpenter, is not supposed to run an extension cord or plug in his own equipment. That's the electrician's job. I know it sounds petty, but the electrician is responsible for all the electrical equipment on the jobsite. If something goes wrong or doesn't work right, or worse, someone gets hurt, it's the electricians fault. So I walked over to him and asked him what he was doing. He explained that the electricians were short-handed and he had been waiting forty-five minutes. He wanted to get his job done by the end of the day but couldn't because all the electricians were backed up. He told me that he went to his truck and got his own drill, which hadn't been used and had been sitting there for about a year. And worse than that, it hadn't been safety checked.

I said to him, "Look, Never Dull, you know better than to bring your personal tools onto the jobsite without the electrician looking at it. Especially one that hadn't been safety checked. But since it's already"—I looked at my watch—"sixteen thirty, and cleanup is in thirty minutes ..." I paused and then said, "Let me see it."

I took his drill to do a visual inspection, and the strangest thing happened. As I pulled the trigger, I saw a flash out of the corner of my eye. It sounds strange, even now as I write it down and see it in print, but I could have sworn I saw a woman's face in the light. For just a split second she almost looked like this girl I had a crush on in high school. Sarah was the cheerleading captain, on varsity track, captain of the swim team, the lead in all the school plays all four years, a straight-A student, and head of the honor society. I can still see her, a very beautiful redhead with the brightest blue eyes I had ever seen.

In this flash of light, her hair was flowing like there was a small breeze from somewhere, and she smiled the most beautiful smile I have ever seen. I know, I know, how did I see all of that in just a flash? I don't know, but it was like time stood still for just that moment.

Let me just say I'm a happily married man with three great kids and a dog who thinks she is one of the kids. And my wife, Amanda, my high school sweetheart, she and I have been through a lot and have been married for more than fifteen years. It hasn't all been a bed of roses, we've had our problems. Between money arguments, time not spent with the kids, trying to stay connected to each other, and the short stay I had in the navy (with me being away on nine-month deployments), I mean ... well ... it has been enough to stretch the limits of any marriage. But we managed to work things through, we take care of our children above anything else, and we take care of each other before anything outside the house. Even though I don't fantasize about other women, this "image" really touched me. Then, in a split second, I thought, *What would it have been like if I had chosen Sarah?*

Anyway, like I was saying, I have Bobby's drill in my hand, and after fifteen years in the construction field, and out of habit, I pulled the trigger without thinking about it. Holding that drill was like holding a pen—you can't help but click it open and closed a few times, or like a pencil you tap like a drumstick to a good song.

As I was pulling the trigger and saw this image, I turned to get a better look but then realized I could not let go of the trigger. Like I said, the drill had been in the back of the truck for about a year, but what I didn't notice was the wire was splitting. I was standing on the wire next to the outlet with my left foot, which my boot had picked up a thumb tack and pushed its way into the steel shaft of my safety boot. As I held the drill in my right hand and stood on the cord with my left foot, when I pulled the trigger, the electricity traveled from my left foot to my right hand, across my heart. I saw the bright *flash*—and then it was lights out.

After the initial electric shock, I felt like I was floating and could hear a lot of voices all around me, some female and some male. Some voices from my past and some that sounded like they were from the jobsite. Some sounded official while some sounded like I was in a … bar maybe? It was all jumbled, not really understanding all of it, but understanding some of it, making out some conversations I'd had in the past.

Then it all started to clear and the many voices started to become one … one sweet female voice like someone from a Disney movie. "Are you okay?" I heard over the running of water from a faucet.

"What did you do to me, Amanda?" I heard myself say.

"Amanda? I'm Sarah, your wife, remember? You must have hit your head harder than I thought. I told you not to stretch farther than you needed to, but what do I know?"

Wife? I opened my eyes and saw that I was on a couch in a small living room in a log home. I looked around and saw a fireplace with a fire going, a few chairs, an end table, and a fallen ladder. The voice had come from the kitchen behind the couch.

"Uh, hello?" I said, kind of confused.

"Yes, silly, I'm still here. Who's Amanda? Are you okay?"

"What happened?" I asked.

"I'm not sure," she said over the running water. "I was here in the kitchen cooking tonight's dinner for your parents, and I heard you yell, and then there was a crash. I came in and saw you on the floor and a little blood on the cornerstone of the fireplace. I went to get Brad from next door to help put you on the couch, and he went to call Dr. Chris."

The faucet stopped, and then I heard footsteps.

"To tell you the truth, I thought you were"—she paused, and then I saw her—"dead" she finished.

Suddenly I had tunnel vision, with her face in the middle of it. It was her, the woman I'd seen just as I got zapped. How did I know her? I mean, she looked familiar, but who was she?

She walked over, put a wet washcloth on my head, knelt next to me, and said, "Just relax; everything is going to be all right. Do you remember anything?"

"Well," I said, "I was standing there on the jobsite talking to Bobby—"

She interrupted. "Jobsite? Who's Bobby?"

I hesitated. "I'm not sure. I guess I had one of those dreams that seemed so real."

"Well, you'd better be all right. It's already 4:30—no, wait, 4:31. If you're still sitting on that couch when your dad gets here, you'll have to explain to him what happened, and then you know that will just kick up an argument about you doing things on your own in your condition."

My first thought was, my parents? My parents died in a car accident when a drunk driver smashed into them about seventeen years ago. It was the same afternoon, despite my being very nervous, I remember asking Sarah out to the fall dance at school and her turning me down. Then, later on, as my friends and I were showing off, I ran my bicycle into a tree in front of the Pizza Palace, and Amanda saw the accident and ran out to see if I was okay, which is how we met. I gave her my phone number, and she ran into the Pizza Palace to call my parents and told them to meet us at the hospital. Then she called her dad and he drove us to the hospital. My parents were hit only three miles from the emergency room. I didn't get the news until two hours later when I was trying to sign out.

And what did Sarah mean by "my condition"?

"I think I'm starting to feel better." I handed her the towel and sat up. "I'm gonna put the ladder away and get ready for tonight. Do you need any help in the kitchen?"

She smiled a most beautiful smile, kissed me ever-so-gently on the cheek, and said in the sweetest voice, "Aww, isn't that nice. You're still trying to take care of me after all this time. Thanks, but I'm almost ready. Here, stay seated for a moment." She handed me back the wet towel for my head.

"No, I'm okay. Let me …"

As I was putting the washcloth down on the arm of the couch, some guy busted open the front door and ran in, out of breath. "Doc's on his way," he said in a hurry, but then relaxed, and with some concern, said, "Hey, you'd better lay back down. That was some fall you took. How's the ol' noggin?" he said, pointing to his own head.

"Thanks, Brad!" Sarah called out.

So that's Brad from next door, I thought.

"I'm fine, worrywart. You shouldn't have bothered the doc on his day off." Then I thought, *How did I know this doctor, and how did I know it was his day off?* Something strange was going on.

"No bother," came a voice from behind Brad. "I've always got time for my most important patient."

Patient? What's going on here? I thought.

Dr. Chris, an older man with white in both his very full head of hair and on his face, walked in from behind Brad and crossed the room. He knelt next to me and said, "Now let's have a look. Follow my finger … good. Let me see that bump. That's going to be some knot on the back of your head for a couple of days, but nothing a hat won't cover up. At least it stopped bleeding. How do you feel? What do you remember?"

"Well, I think I was changing the lightbulb, and instead of moving the ladder over a couple of inches, I reached for the second light and … I guess I lost my balance."

"I told him not to reach, but does he listen to me?" Sarah said, shaking her head, looking at me with frustration.

"Now we talked about this before," Doc said sternly. "No more leaving the floor. That vertigo you got from the transient ischemic attack, and then the stroke at work … it's going to be the end of you. That's why you had to move the bedroom down to the main floor, because of the stairs. Now ladders? What are you thinking?"

"He thought he was on a 'jobsite' with someone named … Bobby?" Sarah said, a little concerned, looking at the doctor.

"Bobby? Jobsite? Your brain is trying to ease you into a more comfortable direction. With the trauma from the fall, your mind must have tried to take you somewhere else to reduce the pain. Do you remember anything else?" Doc asked, resting his jaw on both thumbs with his fingers intertwined and forefingers pointing up.

"No, I really don't even remember that. It seems more like a dream now."

"Well, like I said," Doc said as he lowered his hands and stood up, "when this happens, write it down in that book I gave you. It may not seem like a big deal now, but it might help out later."

"Thanks for stopping by. I've got to get ready for tonight," I said as I got up off the couch, having to grab the armrest for support.

Doc and Sarah grabbed one arm each to help steady me, and Brad stood in front of me to catch me if I started to tip over.

Still holding my arm and looking at me, Doc said, "Hey, that's right! Tonight's the dinner with the parents, right? Let me know how it goes." And then, leaning forward in front of me to talk to Sarah, he said, "Sarah, behave yourself. Don't go off half-cocked. All right?" He shook his finger from his free hand at her like a little kid.

"Yes, Dr. Chris. You'll be the first one we tell our story to," Sarah said with a smile, shaking her head and looking up.

As I stood there under my own power, Doc and Sarah slowly let go but did not move away. Brad backed completely out of the way, and all three watched me like I was some baby learning to walk.

I took a step or two by myself and noticed the sunlight streaming through the sliding glass door to my right. I walked over to it and looked outside. I saw a porch just outside the glass door with an armchair to the left of the door. Past the railing was a row of treetops, and just beyond that was a beautiful lake that we were above, high on a hillside. The setting sunlight was dancing around the lake like lights off a diamond facet. I heard a motorboat somewhere off in the distance and the sounds of birds and crickets.

I turned back around to see Brad and Doc just to the side of the light coming in through the window, so only Sarah was in the golden glow of the setting sun by herself. She was more beautiful than just five minutes ago, if that was even possible. Though I could not hear what they were talking about, her voice was soothing, and her skin looked so soft. When she smiled her cheeks shined, her dimples were deep, and her eyes sparkled. She had on a flowery summer dress, and as she stood there in the light, she kind of swung so that her dress moved back and forth. As she was talking and laughing with the two gentlemen, I couldn't stop staring at her. Then, without turning her head, she looked at me, and I really thought she was an angel who came down from heaven to save me.

"Why are you staring at me?" she asked, smiling even bigger and still moving back and forth. Brad and Dr. Chris stopped talking and turned toward me.

"I was just thinking … thinking … umm … I have to get ready for dinner."

Sarah looked at her watch and said, "Hey, you're right. Sorry, guys, the chitchat is over. We have guests coming." And she shooed them out the front door.

At first I felt like I was in someone else's body and not in control. How did I know where the bedroom was or where my clothes were? But as I went through the motions, my other life seemed to fade.

After a hot shower, the other life became the dream and this one my real life, the one that was meant to be. Sarah and I did not talk while we were getting ready and hardly said a word to each other before my parents showed up. She looked stunning in her pastel-pink dinner dress, not really a summer dress and not really an evening gown. And it was only the fourth one she tried on. She tried on the first one and asked me what I thought, and I said she looked great, but then she said the neckline was too low. She tried on the second one and asked me again what I thought, and I said she looked great, but then she said the sleeves were too short. The third one was too long after I said it looked great. Finally she tried on the fourth one but did not ask my opinion.

I said, "Why didn't you ask what I thought?"

She replied, "Oh, you're no help; you like everything."

No sooner did we get into the living room than the front doorbell rang. It was Mom and Dad. We both walked over to the door. Sarah looked in the mirror one more time and said something about her hair. I took her by the hand as she tried to run past me, and I said, "Honey, you look beautiful, really." And I kissed her hand.

She smiled and took her other hand, placed it on my cheek, and said, "That was very nice. Are you going to let them in?"

"Right, let them in," I said, letting go of her hand. I opened the door, and there they were. I didn't even feel surprised to see them there, right in front of me, alive. It was the most natural thing in the world. They came in, and we talked for about an hour about the house, work, and the weekend.

Dad and I went out on the deck and watched the fading sunlight pass over the lake on the far side. The girls set the table, and then we were called for dinner. We seemed to eat and talk for hours. Finally it was time for them to go. I gave Mom a big hug and shook my dad's hand, just like I always did, and said our good nights, and the two of us waved to them from the front porch as they drove out the driveway.

We walked back in the house and sat on the couch. Sarah let out a big sigh of relief and put her feet up on my lap. "I think that went well."

I looked at her, with the curls still set in the front part of her hair, her face still glowing, and the smell of her perfume still fresh. I started to say "I … I … love y—" but the room started to spin, and then I heard …

*

"Honey? Nurse, get the doctor. I think he's coming around!" It was a different voice and sounded like it was in the distance.

"Where am I?" I asked, a little groggy.

"You're in St. Peter's Hospital, honey. Are you okay? The kids and I have been really worried. It's been a week since we got the call. We all thought you were—"

"Dead?" I heard myself say. I opened my eyes and said, "Amanda? Is that really you?"

Of course it is, silly. Who else would it be?"

"Amanda … am I glad to see you. I had a … strange … dream," I said as I tried to sit up.

"You stay right where you are, young man," came a voice from the opening door. I looked up, and a doctor was coming into the almost empty room, just the three of us and an empty bed to my right, next to the window. For some reason, I noticed the room number on the door as he walked in, 1632, which seemed strange at the time.

I said, "Dr. Chris?"

The older man with white in both his very full head of hair and on his face, a white lab coat, and a stethoscope around his neck said, "Why, yes. Have we met before?"

"Only in a dream, I think ... only in a dream."

"Well, that's interesting. I understand you were electrocuted. Do you feel well enough to tell me about it?"

I went through the day's events and just skipped over seeing the girl's face in a flash and the whole different multidimensional thing.

"I saw the flash, and then I was here," I said, hoping no one would ask me for more detail. Then I added hopefully, "When can I go home, Doc?"

"Well ... I'd like to keep you here for some more tests, but it's really up to you," Doc Chris said with just his eyes looking up from the chart. "But if you go home, you should stay in bed for at least twenty-four hours to make sure there aren't any side effects."

"What should we look for, Doctor?" Amanda asked quietly.

"Well, there's dehydration, weakness, sensitivity to light, dizziness, and maybe some loss of appetite. If you have the time, Amanda, you should stay with him at least for the day to watch over him."

"What about, oh, I don't know, strange … dreams?" I asked, half not wanting to.

"*Strange dreams* can sometimes be an outlet of regrets in our lives. You should write everything down and keep a running log of these events."

"Yeah, that's what you said last time," I said in a low voice.

"What was that?" he asked with a confused look.

"What did you say, honey?" Amanda asked, rubbing my arm.

"I said … that … we're getting out of here at a good time. *No* traffic."

"Oh," said the doctor, half-believing me. "Well, if you need me, I'll be here at the hospital, or call and they'll know how to get in touch with me. Take it easy," he said as he finished writing on the clipboard and then left the room.

Amanda started to run her long fingers through my hair with one hand and rubbed my arm with the other and just stared at me.

"Where are the kids?" I asked.

"They're with Jenny, the sitter from two doors down. How do you feel? Do you want to stay the night here?"

"Are you kidding? Let's see … stay here and get a good night's sleep with those really cute nurses who come in and check on me *every* hour, or go home to a house with three screaming kids, a barking dog, that dripping faucet, and who knows what else. Ummmm, let me think."

There was a moment of silence, and then at the same time, we both said, "Home it is."

I was up and dressed in no time at all. Amanda went to get the car while I checked out of the hospital. I still could not shake the feeling that something was wrong. I signed the last piece of paper, and the nurse told me I had to leave the hospital in a wheelchair, hospital rules. I didn't really feel like arguing, so I sat in the wheelchair and waited for my wife.

At the far end of a hallway, large windows faced the west, and the sun was just off the horizon and going down. It was a deep orange color and made everything in the hallway look almost golden. I was trying to remember when I saw a glow like that before. I was looking at everything in the hallway, from the pictures of mountains, lakes, and farmland to the checked pattern of the installed couches that lined both sides of the hallway. I looked out the window, admiring the wonder of it all when a nurse came into the hallway, way down by the window.

From this distance, she was just a silhouette, but she seemed to move slowly, like in a movie, very sexy. I look down at my hands to not seem like I was staring but could still hear the soft tap of her shoes as she walked toward me.

Then a soft voice beside me said, "Here we go," and I heard the release of the brake on the wheel to my right. I looked up, and in the window from the north wing, I saw my wife driving up from the parking lot.

I said, "I'm ready."

She wheeled me down the hallway and out the front door. All the while I was having this strange feeling that something was not like it was suppose to be. Everything seemed like it was going in slow motion. I remember the car pulling up and Amanda coming around the car, saying, "I can't believe it's already 4:34 in the afternoon. Where does the time go?"

The nurse said, "*Are* you ready to go?" I looked over and saw a very pretty redhead with blue eyes locking the wheels and then helping me out of the wheelchair by grabbing my right arm.

As I was getting up, I looked at her and said, "Don't I know you from somewhere?"

Then, as Amanda grabbed my left arm, it was like electricity going from my left side to my right. Then in a flash of light I heard in a very faint voice, "Yes, you do."

Then … darkness!

In the darkness, the voices were all around me again. Some sounded familiar, some strange. Some seemed to echo, while others were barely audible. Then I heard faint crying, almost childlike. I felt like I was floating through the air, not really falling, not really flying.

Then without warning, I felt a breeze blow across my face. At first it was light and almost refreshing. Then it started to blow a little harder and began to swirl all around me, causing a tornado kind of effect. It was kind of scary and exhilarating at the same time. Then I landed with a thud.

"Where am I?"

"You're at the hospital waiting for your checkup, *again*." I heard a voice say.

"Amanda?" I said softly.

"Who is this 'Amanda'? You asked for her a couple of months ago when we were at home," a shocked voice echoed.

My eyes shot open. "Sarah? How long have we waiting?" I then noticed we were sitting in the hallway of the hospital just outside Dr. Chris's office.

"Who is *Amanda*?" she said, a little more sternly.

"Oh … Sarah … sorry … she is … she is just the night nurse here, I told you about her last time," I managed to say. And then said a little softer, "How long have we been here?"

Her face stayed stern for a moment longer and then melted into the caring beauty I remembered. "I'm sorry. I just hate when we have to keep coming back here. How do you feel?"

I looked around the hall trying to get a feel of how much time had passed and something felt … odd. "Sarah, what's today?"

Sarah smiled that beautiful smile and said, "Today's Tuesday the twelfth. Are you all right?"

"Oh, right, the twelfth of September," I said, a little confused.

She said, "No, the twelfth of December. Honestly, I really don't know where your head is sometimes. What would you do without me, I wonder. I think I'll get you a calendar for Christmas after all."

"Right, right. That's what I meant. The twelfth of De-cem-ber. I was thinking of something else. What time is it anyway, dear?"

"*Wow.* Dear, is it? I really cannot remember the last time you called me that. And you said it this time without cringing. I guess there's hope for you yet. Hmm … it's about 4:35 in the afternoon. Why? Do you have a date?"

"Is it 'about' or is it 4:35?"

"What's going on? Why is the time so important?"

"I … umm … it's the … the doc … he told me to write everything down, that's all. I have to write the time down also, to keep … you know … better track. That's all."

She smiled a little, sat up straight, and said, "The exact time, according to my watch, is 4:36 in the afternoon on the twelfth of December 2013."

December 2013? I thought. *Where did the last year go? I really don't understand. It seems that only last week I was on the jobsite looking at a drill. I really don't want to upset her any more, so I'll just play along.*

"Is there anything I can get you while we wait for Dr. Chris?" she asked after about ten minutes. "I hope he gets here soon. We have to get home to feed the cat and then go to bed because I have to get up early tomorrow for a meeting with the realtor about the house next door."

"That sounds familiar. I'm sorry, I forgot to ask. Did you pass your realtor's test?" I asked a little quietly, not sure if I should even ask, and then I thought, *We have a* cat? *That can't be right. I'm a dog person.*

"Yes I did, I passed the written exam last Monday. This will be my final test before I go out on my own, and luckily it happens to be right next door."

There was a moment of silence, and then I said, "That's great. I'm really proud of you. I'm sure you'll do well with the sale."

Sarah smiled and returned to her normal glow. She stood from her chair next to me and leaned over and kissed me on the forehead. She combed my hair with her fingernails a few times and then said, "I'll be right back. Do you want something to drink? Hot or cold?"

"Cold. Definitely *cold*."

She looked at me for a long minute, almost like she wanted to say something else but didn't know how. Then she turned and walked down the hallway. She took about a dozen steps, stopped, and turned around. She opened her mouth just a little and paused one more time. She closed it and smiled that beautiful smile and turned back around. Before she could finish turning, Dr. Chris came around the corner and almost walked right into her. Sarah jumped back with a little shriek.

"Oh, I'm sorry, I didn't see you. Are you all right?" asked Dr. Chris.

"You almost got me, Dr. Chris. *Almost*. I was just going for something to drink. Would you like something? And would you make sure he doesn't leave without me, please?" Sarah asked him but was looking at me.

"I thought he would be sleeping in that chair by now. That's why I hurried back to check up on him. You go on now; I'll take care of him." He stepped aside and let her finish walking down the hallway.

Sarah kissed her hand and blew it toward me. I pretended to catch it, something I don't *ever* remember doing before. Possibly a show for Dr. Chris.

She smiled and walked away. Doc looked at me and said, "Come on in," and we walked into his office.

He walked in first and stood by the door. As I walked in, I noticed the exam table, a counter with medical stuff on it, and a window with the closed curtains.

He closed the door. Dr. Chris walked past me to the counter and picked up a clipboard, turned to me as he pointed to the exam table, and said, "Please jump up here, would you, so I can check you out."

I stepped up on the pull-out step and sat on the table. He put the clipboard under his arm, picked up my hand, felt my wrist, and said, "So how are you feeling today at"—he looked at his watch—"four thirty-seven? Are you warm, cold, hungry, or thirsty?"

"You know, Doc, that's the funny thing. I don't think I've eaten in days, but I'm not hungry or even thirsty. Why is that? In fact, I feel like I am going a little … I don't know …"

"Crazy?" Doc said, letting go of my wrist and writing down some numbers on the clipboard.

"I was going to say 'not myself,' but maybe your word is a better way I'm feeling."

He looked at me for a moment. He put down the clipboard and said as compassionately as he could, "Do you think you want to try to talk about it? I'm done with my rounds and have about a half hour to spend with you, if you want to try."

I thought about it for a moment and then said, "You know, I think I would like that very much."

Doc sat on the table next to me and said, "Why don't you start from where you want to … five minutes ago, five days ago, or even twenty years ago. Wherever you want."

I sat there swinging my feet for a moment, watching them go back and forth, getting my thoughts together, wondering if I should tell him the whole thing or not, wondering if he would even believe me.

Then he said, "Go ahead, tell me the whole thing and don't worry whether I'll believe you."

My eyes darted up to stare at him.

He continued, "Tell me about the last year, if that's where you want to start. Sometimes just saying things out loud can make *you* feel better, even if no else believes you. It might even help you with your priorities on what you should do, like where to go next. How you should complete your, shall we say, your next phase of life."

Was he really reading my mind, or was this just a really weird coincidence? There was something about him that I just couldn't put my finger on. There was something strange, yet something comfortable about talking to him, like talking to an old friend or close relative. Someone you can trust with anything. But still, I felt like I shouldn't put all my cards on the table … not yet, anyway. I felt like I had to finish something else first.

"You know what …" I whispered. "I'm feeling tired all of a sudden. I think I'd like a rain check on that talk, if it's all right with you, Doc."

Dr. Chris looked down at the floor for a moment, like he'd just dropped something, and then looked back at me and said with a forced smile, "That's okay. When you're ready, I'll be around. But you shouldn't wait too long. The mind can play nasty little tricks, making it hard to tell the difference between right and wrong, good and bad, or even good and evil. I'll be around to help you when you're ready." With that, he jumped off the table, patted me on the back, and started for the door.

Not knowing if I should say anything, I said, "Hey, Doc?"

He stopped and turned around and looked at me, raised his eyebrows, and said "Yes?"

I took a moment and said, "Am I okay? I mean … the checkup. Can I leave?"

He smiled and said, "You're fine. But think about what I said. *Seriously* think about what I said. And like I said, we all go through life just once. Make the most of it."

I said, "Is this real? I mean, right now, this very minute, is this … *real*?"

He took the pen out of his pocket, looked at it for a moment, tossed it to me, and said, "It's as real as you make it."

I watched the pen float through the air, and when I caught it, I looked up and saw the door closing. Doc was gone.

Sarah came back to the office with two drinks, and we left the hospital. She drove, and as I sat in the passenger's seat looking out the window, I really thought about what Doc Chris said, trying to make sense of the whole day … the past year, for that matter.

That night after we got into bed, I kissed Sarah good night and again could not believe how beautiful she was. Like time somehow stood still for just her. I shut off the light and just laid there, thinking. It took a while for me to fall asleep, but when I did it was not an easy sleep. I dreamed of my past. At first it was of when I was a young boy playing without a care in the world. Playing ball with my friends, going to the beach with my family, I even dreamed of little Donna Markenson and how I wanted to spend the rest of my life with her, only to have that feeling last just one school year. I dreamed of my dad showing me how to work on the car, build models, and practice wood carving. I dreamed of my mom teaching me how to cook, do laundry, and clean the house.

Then my dreams took a turn for the worse. I dreamed about my uncontrolled, troubled teen years. From stealing my first piece of candy to the third jacket I swiped that landed me in police custody from the Get-It-Here store that was locally owned by a very nice family. I dreamed about when my dad had to come and pick me up from the police station, and the look of discontent he had for me, and all I did was act like I didn't care, but it was really eating me up inside. I was dreaming of all the things I did wrong and was feeling very bad for what I had put my parents through, when I noticed a dark shadow following me. I started to run, and it seemed to chase me. I ran toward a light in the distance, and then it stopped following me. All of a sudden, I woke up to the morning light coming in through the window.

"Come on, sleepyhead, you're going to be late for your son's graduation," Amanda said.

"What ... what are you talking about?" I said, rubbing my eyes. I looked around. I was in my own bed, and Amanda was opening the curtains to let in the sunlight.

"Graduation ... son ... today? Let's go. Honestly, sometimes it's like you don't even listen to what I say anymore." Amanda seemed a little frustrated.

"I'm sorry, did you say something, dear?" I said, still rubbing my eyes, peeking through my hands at her.

Amanda turned around and gave me one of those looks that she gives the kids when they try to mouth off to her.

I dropped my hands. "Oh, *that* graduation," I said as she turned back to the window. "I thought you were talking about another graduation. Oh, yeah, of course I know about *our* son's graduation. What, you think I could forget about a thing like that? Oh, you silly woman."

Amanda stopped opening the curtains and stood there for a moment. In the sunlight she looked more ... lovely, I guess. Maybe more beautiful would be a better way to put it. She looked—I don't know—not just older but more mature, I think. But then she slowly turned around and stared at me and said in a low, growling voice, "Why, you big faker." And in one fell swoop, she picked up a pillow and hit me with it before I could say anything else.

We were still laughing when the boys came running into the room asking what happened. All Amanda could say after hitting me a couple of more times was, "Your father is just being ... well ... your father." She threw the pillow at me one more time as she walked out of the room yelling, "One hour—that's it. We're leaving in one hour. *All* of us."

I looked at the boys and shrugged.

Tommy looked at me and said, "What did you do this time to get her so riled up?"

"*Me?* Whose side are you on?" I said as I threw the pillow at him. Tommy ducked, and the pillow hit Brian right in the face.

From downstairs, we could hear Amanda yell, "Fifty-five minutes. We will not be late. Got it?"

"That's my cue to get up, I think," I said as I threw back the covers and jumped out of bed.

Tommy said, "That just might be the best decision you'll make all day." I grabbed another pillow, and both boys ran out of the room pushing each other and ducking their heads.

I got up, got dressed in a suit and tie, and went downstairs for breakfast.

We all ate pretty quickly and were in the car, backing down the driveway, when Amanda said, "Very good, five minutes to spare."

I said as I put my hand down on the center console, "Five minutes? I could still put away some tools."

Tommy said, "And I could feed the dog again."

Brian piped up with, "That's enough time to put away my bike."

And then Joann added, "I could still do the dishes."

"That's enough from the peanut gallery. See what you started?" she said to me, pointing her finger at me. She lowered her hand and placed it on mine. Then she turned, looked out the window, and under her breath said, "Troublemaker." We all started to laugh.

We got to the high school in plenty of time. Tommy went to his classroom to meet up with his friends and put on his graduation gown, and we went to the auditorium.

As we walked in, Dr. Chris was standing off to the side talking with one of the parents. When he saw us, he excused himself and walked over to us. He stuck out his hand and said, "I'm glad you could make it. I heard you weren't feeling well. I was going to stop by the house after this shindig. You know it's been six years almost to the day of the accident. How are you doing?"

"Six years, really? It seems like only last week." I excused myself from the family, kissed Amanda on the cheek, and whispered, "I'll be right back." She nodded, and I turned to the doc and said, "Do you have a minute?"

He smiled and said, "For you, I have two."

We walked a couple of steps away to the wall as my family walked to their seats.

At first I just looked at the carpet, and then I looked right into his eyes and said, "I'd like to talk to you about … well … some stuff that's been going on. When would be a good time to see you?"

"I'll be at the hospital tomorrow. The new one. I finally moved out of the old one a few months ago."

"But that's imposs—wait. You said it's been six years since the accident. Wow, time really did go fast."

"Faster than you think. Don't take it for granted. Whatever you need to do in life, you really should do it, before it's too late. Come see me tomorrow; don't put it off. Now, let's watch Tommy and his friends graduate."

The ceremony went great. Amanda and Joann cried, Brian made faces at Tommy, and I thought about what I was going to say to the doc.

After it was over, we stood around congratulating the other parents and talked about the kids' futures.

After about a half hour, Amanda whispered in my ear, "I am going to take the kids to the car. We'll wait for you there. Try not to be too long," and then she kissed me on the cheek.

I looked at her and nodded. I turned back to Wendy and Bob Hicks, whose daughter just graduated with Tommy. After about five minutes, we said good-bye and good luck to the kids, and I turned and walked up the aisle. I remember thinking about how much time had passed since the accident. I remember reaching for the door handle and turning it to leave the auditorium, and then with a deep breath, I pushed the door open—only to have it open onto the fourth floor of the construction site where Bobby was working in the middle of the floor, and I saw him plugging in a drill. Someone stood beside him.

I turned around and saw the stairwell of the construction site. Now I was really confused. The guy standing next to Bobby was dressed like me. Though his back was toward me, he looked familiar. I saw him talking to Bobby, and then I saw a drill in his hand. I started toward him when all of a sudden I saw this dark shadow coming up from the street side of the floor. At first it didn't seem to know I was there, and I kept moving toward Bobby and this man. As I started to run to the center of the room, where the two men stood to warn them, the shadow noticed me and started to move toward them more quickly. I was about five steps away when I saw this man raise the drill and pull the trigger. All at once I got that same feeling across my chest as I did six years ago. The pain in my chest, the cringing of my hands and legs, the flashing of people in my life—and then I fell to the ground.

Next thing I knew, I was sitting up in my bed, dripping wet from sweat and gasping for air. A voice in the darkness said, "Not again. Are you all right?"

It sounded familiar, but this time, I didn't blurt out a name. "Yeah, yeah. Just that dream again. Just that … dream … again," I said, wiping my face on my already wet T-shirt. "Sorry to wake you up."

"Oh, *that's all right*. I mean, it's almost time to get up, anyway," she said as the light came on. It was Sarah. "I mean, it's *only*"—she looked at the clock—"four forty-seven. And since the alarm was gonna go off at five …"

"Why do you do that? You always seem to make a case out of everything I do. What did I do to make you have so much animosity toward me?" I said in a low voice.

"Animosity? Do you really want to have this talk again? Look, for the millionth time, when you asked me out to the fall dance back in high school and I said yes, it wasn't because I wanted to go with you in particular. It was just that no one else asked me to go. Me! I had so much going for me that all the guys were either afraid to ask or just assumed I had already been asked to the dance … or a movie … or just to go to the local pizza place just to hang out, for that matter. And then *you* came along, all scared and all. But then you—*you*—somehow got up the nerve to ask me to the dance. I said yes because I wanted to show everyone else that I could be fun and have a good time with everyone else. You were so nice and treated me so well, the way I should be treated, you'd said. After a couple of years of 'begging,' I said yes to your marriage proposals because I figured that was my ticket out of that town. When my dad hired you, and you got that office job downtown, I thought that was my way up. I mean, *our* way up. You help me, and I help you. You got a job with a corner office, and I got a lifestyle I could live with. A win-win situation. Don't get me wrong; I really do appreciate everything you've done for me, but honestly, you were not my first choice," she finished, and she rolled over to face the wall.

I sat there for a few minutes and tried to remember our life together. The memories slowly started coming to me. I saw myself asking her to the dance, and then fast-forward to me proposing to her at the Jersey shore. A few years after that I got promoted at work. During that time, I was working sometimes eighteen-, nineteen-hour days, and I guess that's where I started to lose … *me*! Between feeling trapped in the marriage and the stress of the job, it started to take its toll, and I started to suffer a physical breakdown. That must be why I became Dr. Chris's "favorite patient."

But why didn't she seem to grow older? How was it that she still looked good … no, better than in high school? Though somehow I knew better than to ask, I said, "And how is it you never seem to get any … older?" Then I felt like I really didn't want to know.

She let out a loud breath and slowly turned over to face me again. Then she … smiled and said in a soft voice, "Thank you. I guess that's why I have stayed with you all these years. You make me feel so—I don't know—special, I guess. You have always—and I mean *always*—put me first in anything you do. That's why I take care of myself … for you. Well, me and Dr. Green, that is."

"Dr. Green?" I said, a little confused.

"Yes, silly, my plastic surgeon."

"But you're the most beautiful woman I've ever met. Why do you need a plastic surgeon?"

"Look, if this is going to be about money again, you can go and sleep in the guest room," she said, a little agitated.

"No, it's not about money," I said a little louder. "What I mean is, isn't that like false advertising? Why can't you just be happy with who *you* are? Grow old gracefully and be happy with your age?"

"Because 'old' people finish last," she blurted. "Do you see the way older people are treated around here? Sure,

I know all about what they've done for us and all their contributions and all, but no one wants them around. I don't want to end up like that. And then kids act like the elderly are not that important and only people to go to see every once in a while for the day. I remember when I was a kid, we went to see my grandma once, sometimes twice, a year. All she wanted to do was cook and tell me what's wrong with the world today and how great the *old days* were. I was kind of glad when she passed. Then Mom, Dad, and I didn't have to go and drive those six hours to spend three hours because she got tired of us being there."

"Speaking of kids," I said a little quieter, "I was wondering ..."

"If you're thinking of having any, I think you picked the wrong person. We both have our careers that keep us busier than who knows what. Not to mention we aren't spring chickens anymore, buddy boy," she said with a bit of disdain.

"Why can't you ... you ... go ... and ... be ..."

I heard Sarah's voice start to fade as she said, "I think you're having another attack." Then the room went dark.

As the dark gave way to gray, I felt someone's hand on my shoulder gently shaking me. "Dad, *Dad*? Are you awake? I have to go."

Go? Who's going? And why? Wait, I remember. "Huh? Oh, I'm sorry. I must have fallen asleep. What time is it?" I asked, looking up at my son Brian, who now seemed to be a young man in his late teens with his hair combed neatly and wearing his light-blue golf shirt and khaki Dockers.

"Yeah, that chair will knock you out fast if you're not careful. If you don't want to take me to the bus stop, I can ask Mom."

"No, no. I told you I'd take you, and I will. Just give me a moment to wake up. Are you ready for this?"

"I guess as ready as I'll ever be. Do you think I'm making the right decision, Dad?"

Suddenly I felt very much awake. "I think we are beyond what I think here. But I am very proud of you. You have made a decision to make something with your life and are following it through by getting on that bus. That's better than half the people you graduated with have done. You are going to do more, see more, and experience more than almost all those people in your first year in the navy than they will their entire lifetime. You are a very smart person, and we aren't too worried about you. You know who you can talk to and who you can trust. Just remember all those tedious things your mom and I taught you, like doing as you're told, cleaning up after yourself—and what's that other thing we're always pushing on you …?"

"Manners?" Brian said with a half smile.

"That's it. Manners. Very good. But above all else, you have to remember one thing. If you forget everything else, always remember one thing."

"What's that?" Brian said, kind of confused.

"Always remember that your mom and I are very proud of you and love you very much."

As I stood up, Brian gave me a big hug.

As we stood there for a moment, Amanda came in and asked, "Is everything okay?"

I looked at her and smiled and said, "I was just telling him how proud of him we are."

Like turning on a faucet, Amanda's eyes filled with tears. She walked over and joined in our little hug.

I looked at my watch and said, "Hey, we have to get going or you'll miss your bus to meet up with your recruiter."

We broke up our little group hug, and I grabbed the car keys, and Brian grabbed his backpack. Amanda called for Joann and the two of them waved as Brian and I got in the car and started to drive to the bus stop.

On the way, we talked about small things. Funny things that had happened, things that might have happened differently, and the next thing we knew, we were at the bus stop. I parked, and as we got out, Brian took his backpack from the backseat and slowly closed the door. He opened his mouth to say something, but then closed it and just stared at me.

I walked around to his side and put my arm around his shoulders and said, "Yes, I think you're doing the right thing. It might be the best decision you will ever make in your life. Go have fun. Meet new people. Experience new things. But most importantly, live your life to the fullest. Don't forget to write to your mom every once in a while. She'll like that."

Brian smiled.

We walked to the bus stop without another word and waited only a few minutes before the bus arrived. The doors opened, and I looked at him and shook his hand. He looked at me and hugged me one more time and said, "Thank you. Thank you for everything."

He let go and turned quickly and got on the bus. Once he sat down, the bus doors closed. I waved as the bus pulled away, and as it did, I started to get tunnel vision with the bus in the center of the closing tunnel and then … darkness.

Again, the voices were all around me but somehow seemed to be echoing like in a hallway or a big room. When they started to quiet down, the darkness gave way to a dim light that seemed to be getting brighter. When I could see clearly, I was in a stairwell that was under construction. I turned around and saw a door. As I walked over to it, I could hear voices in a big room and what sounded like a voice on a walkie-talkie. I opened the door and stood in the doorway. In the middle of the room was a bunch of people standing around someone lying down. Two of the people were medics, and they were helping the guy who was lying down. As I looked around, it all seemed familiar. I could see this was some kind of a construction site, just the concrete floor with pillars and another slab above and no walls. There were some guys in work clothes and hardhats with tools standing off to the side, and some guys in suits and hardhats stood closer to the body.

It was late afternoon, and the sun was going down. A warm breeze blew in from the west. As I stood there looking at all that was going on, I noticed a shadow in the corner of the room standing away from the crowd. At first it was barely noticeable, but once I saw it, it became my main focus. I squinted to see it better and then noticed it wasn't standing in the corner, but … floating. It was drifting back and forth in the light breeze. I don't think it noticed me, because it had the full attention of the guy in the middle of the room.

I heard one of the medical guys say to the other, "I think we have him stable enough to move him to the hospital now. Call ahead and let them know we're on our way."

This seemed to upset the shadow because it started to move back and forth faster. Then, as if it had made up its mind, it started to move toward the crowd. I felt like I had to do something. I entered the room and ran toward the shadow, yelling, "Get away, *get away!*"

It heard me, it really heard me. I seemed to have startled it, because it became aware that I was there. It looked from side to side, as if looking for an escape, and then flew off and over the edge of the building toward the east and disappeared.

The crowd moved behind me toward the stairs, carrying the guy on a stretcher. I heard the one medic talking to the hospital on the radio. "We are en route to you now. ETA is ten minutes. Local time, sixteen fifty."

I stood there in the empty room for a couple more seconds thinking something seemed very strange. I could still hear voices in the stairwell until I heard the door shut, then … quiet. Though the breeze was warm, I was starting to feel a little cold. I shivered once and turned for the door. I walked over to it, looked over my shoulder for the shadow one more time, and reached, turned the doorknob, and pushed the door open … right into the front hallway of our home. Straight ahead was the kitchen, and sitting at the table was Amanda with a young couple. Amanda stood up when she saw me, and as she walked toward me, she said, "There you are. We were getting worried about you. We thought you forgot about tonight."

As she walked over to me, I noticed she had aged about fifteen years. Still very beautiful but older.

She kissed me on the cheek, took me by the hand, and walked me to the kitchen. She said, "You were supposed to be home earlier for Joann's big announcement, remember? She has been sitting on pins and needles waiting for you."

"Announcement?" I said in a low voice and a little confused as I put down my briefcase, still walking toward the kitchen. I took off my hat and put it on the end of the banister.

As we walked into the kitchen, the young couple stood up. The boy threw out his hand and with a grin said, "Good evening, sir."

I looked down at his hand, then looked at my wife, then to the young lady, and then to my wife again, as if to say, "What do I do now?"

My wife said, "Dear?" and nodded toward the boy with his hand still out in front of him.

"I … I'm … I'm sorry, long day at work." I said with a nervous laugh as I took his hand. "Good evening to you too, umm …"

"Daaad!" the young lady said. "You know his name is Tony."

"*Tony* … right. Tony. How are you doing this evening, T-O-N-Y." Everyone started to laugh as we stopped shaking hands.

I looked over at the young lady and could still see the little girl who looked over the table and asked if her husband could go to the same college as her. It seemed like only yesterday.

"Okay, what's this 'big' announcement that we need to hear?" I asked after the laughter died down. Joann walked over to the counter and came back with four glasses of what looked like champagne and passed them out. I looked down at the glass and then at her, and I started to open my mouth.

She said, "Sparkling cider, Dad. Just sparkling cider."

I smiled and she continued. "Mom, Dad, Tony and I would like to tell you—"

"Do I need to sit down for this?" I asked, a little shaky.

"*Dad!*" Joann yelled.

"Please, honey—let her finish," Amanda said with the softness of an angel.

"Sorry, sweet pea. Continue," I said in a low voice.

"Tony and I have both been accepted to Yale for next year's session. Isn't that *great?*"

"Now I know I need to sit down," I said and tried to take a sip of my sparkling cider.

Amanda put her hand on my arm and said, "Not yet."

"There's more?" I asked in a voice that was shaky and a little higher than normal.

"Yes, Tony and I would like to tell you that …" In a hurried voice, she said really excitedly, "He asked me to marry him," and threw out her hand with the ring on it.

"Please tell me that's it. I don't know how much more 'good news' I can take in one day," I said, grabbing the chair to help steady me.

"Honey …" Amanda said, giving me a stern look.

"Sorry," I said to Amanda and then looked at Joann. "Sorry, honey. I really am happy for you two. It's just a lot to take in all at once. I mean, just yesterday you were sitting at this very table, barely able to see over it, and now … *now* you are off to college. *And* you're getting *married*! Where did the time go? You were supposed to … I was hoping you would stay my little princess for just a little longer."

With tears welling up in her eyes, Joann managed to say in a calm voice, "But Dad, I will always be your little princess. No matter how old I get. I love you both very much."

And with that, Joann and Amanda broke out into tears as they hugged me.

After about a minute or two of hugging, I looked up at Tony and said, "See what you are getting yourself into?"

Amanda pushed away and Joann gave me a little slap on the arm.

I looked at them and said, "What? He should know!"

We sat there for a few hours just talking. We laughed and told stories to Tony, the newest member of our family, about life in our household.

I asked where the boys were, and Amanda said Tommy was going to try to stop over tonight, but his daughter had a cold and his wife had to work late. Brian was on his way back from a deployment in the South Pacific with the US Navy aboard the USS *Kitty Hawk* and would be in port tomorrow.

As we sat there, I could not help myself from just looking at my beautiful wife and how she seemed to glow as we talked and laughed the night away.

Then, as it usually happens, the talking got less, the laughter subsided to giggles and smiles, and then it was over.

Joann looked at her watch and said, "Wow, is it that late already? I have to go to bed. I have my finals tomorrow."

"Just five more minutes, please?" I pleaded.

"Dad, I really have to get some sleep. Tomorrow after the exams, maybe just you and me. We can go to that diner you like downtown." She kissed me on top of my head as she and Tony started to walk out of the kitchen.

"Promise?" I said, looking up at my little girl.

"Promise," she said with a smile, and they walked out of the room.

We walked them to the front door, and standing there with our arms around each other, Amanda and I waved good night to them as they drove away.

I helped Amanda clean up the kitchen and put things away. We slowly walked through the house, shutting off lights as we walked from room to room without talking.

After I showered, brushed my teeth, and shaved, we laid on the bed. I never noticed before how quiet the house was.

Amanda looked at me and said very softly, "You look like you're carrying the world on your shoulders. What's wrong?" Then she curled up in my arms.

"What could be wrong? Tommy has his family, Brian's in the navy, our little girl is getting married, and we are going to be all alone in this big old house in a couple of months." After a moment of silence, I said, "Let me ask you something, seriously."

"Seriously? Really? You are going to ask me something *seriously*? Let me write this down," she said with a half smile.

"Okay, okay. I guess I deserved that. But let me ask you … have you ever been sorry that I asked you to marry me? Do you have any regrets?"

The room got even quieter; I thought my ears were going to burst. All she did was stare at me. I guess she was trying to see if I was joking again. After what seemed to be hours, she opened her mouth as if to say something and then closed it again like she changed her mind.

I finally said, "You don't have to answer, I was just …"

"Of course I'm going to answer. I'm just trying to find the words to tell you how happy you've made me through all these years. And as far as 'regrets' go, I think I only have one."

My heart sank, and I shifted my position a little farther away from her side. "I understand," I said under my breath.

"No, I don't think you do," she said as her face got serious and she came to rest on her elbow. "The only regret I have is that I didn't start to talk to you sooner than the day of the bicycle accident. I really did want to meet you a lot earlier than that day and with a whole lot less stress than that accident, even if you were showing off for me."

Suddenly I was back in the past, the day of the accident, looking up at Amanda. She was kneeling down on the sidewalk, sitting on her feet (something that still amazes me that anyone can do) with my head on her lap as she combed my hair with her fingers, telling me her dad was on the way and how she had called my parents to meet us at the hospital. She was so calm and caring, I guess it was at that moment I knew I wanted to spend the rest of my life with her.

Then back to the present where she was trying to explain to me how she felt.

"So," I said quietly as I moved closer to her, "you knew I was showing off for you? Why didn't you ever say anything?"

"I don't know," she said as she looked at the ceiling. "I guess I thought it was kind of romantic … I guess." Then she looked right into my eyes and said, "I have always loved you and will always love you no matter where we are or what happens. You will always be the only one for me. And if you go on to the next life before me, know that I will miss you every day until my time comes, and we will be together again."

Our eyes welled up with tears, and we held each other for a long time before we fell asleep.

In my slumber, I dreamed of light and dark, shadows and grays, good and bad between both my worlds. And slowly, like the end of a very bad storm, my thoughts began to clear, and I somehow came to a single thought: that I made the best choice possible for my life and for those around me. I guess you could say that I became at peace with the way my life turned out. At that moment, it was like a cold, wet, heavy blanket was lifted off me, and I could take a much-needed deep breath.

I woke up on my side in a bed feeling a little cold. I looked around only to see that I was in an empty hospital room and Amanda was not next to me. I was dressed in a white hospital gown and no shoes. The room was quiet, but there seemed to be a commotion in the hallway. I slowly got up and walked over to the door. The voices outside the room were getting louder. They sounded like doctors and nurses yelling instruction to other people. Just as I opened the door a little to look out, a bunch of people ran past my door pushing a gurney. There was one doctor on top of the gurney pumping up and down on someone's chest, one person yelling orders, and one person with a clipboard frantically writing things down. Three people walked alongside the gurney, and they looked like they were pushing tubes into this person's arm.

I then noticed the dark shadow following behind everyone. When it saw me, it seemed to be afraid and darted into the opposite wall and disappeared. There was one more medical person walking behind everyone else talking to someone behind him.

"Please wait in the waiting room. As soon as we know something, we'll let you know. *Please* go and sit down. Someone will be with you shortly."

I heard the crowd of doctors hit the double door at the end of the hallway, and then it was quiet again. I opened the door and looked in the hallway, first in the direction of the medical staff. I saw the doors moving back and forth a couple of times. Then I looked in the opposite direction and saw a middle-aged woman with a small child in her arms walking away with two young boys, one on either side. Somehow they looked familiar, and I stepped out of the room toward them.

"Ah … there you are. I've been looking for you, young man," a voice behind me said. The voice startled me enough to make me do a kind of funny dance, like I had just gotten caught with a bag of cookies after bedtime. I turned around really fast to see Dr. Chris looking down at his clipboard.

"Doc, am I glad to see you. I *really* need to talk to you."

"Great. I just happen to have time for you, but we really should hurry. You don't have much time left."

I gave him a strange look and was about to ask what he meant, when he said, "Let's go this way, shall we? I need to check up on someone."

We walked down the hallway toward the double doors. I turned around one more time to see the woman and the three children slowly entering the waiting room with their heads down. "Come on, young man, there really isn't much time left."

We pushed through the double doors and into a hallway with a lot of doors on both sides. Doc turned to me and asked, "So what do you want to talk about?"

"Well, you know I've wanted to talk to you for some time, but I never seemed to know what I wanted to say. I've seen some pretty strange things, and I think I've figured it out. I've always wondered what my life would have been like had I chosen another path. I now realize the path I chose was not only right for me but for others as well. We meet the people we do at a time when they need us or when we need them. Maybe it's all part of a grand design or something."

"And what about when you leave someone?" the doc asked, without looking up from his clipboard.

"I guess that … well … it might be a way of helping you or them to become stronger in another way," I said in a lower voice.

Doc looked at me as he slowly started to walk down the hallway and said, "You don't have much time left, and I want to try and help you make the right choices for yourself right now.

"You had two loves in your life," he continued. "One was in your heart, Amanda. And one was in your head, Sarah. The first time you woke, you were with Sarah in a life you always dreamed about. The beautiful wife, the log home on the lake, no kids, and no dirty construction site to have to go to every day. But in order to get something, you have to give up something. In high school, you knew Sarah to be a very smart person and a great athlete. She was very competitive and motivated in both academics and sports, which transfer over to adulthood where she could use that 'power' on you because you let her. You fed the fire that she needed to feel like someone important, and she fed your fire that you needed to have someone so beautiful.

"When you woke the second time, you were with Amanda. She was always by your side in all that you did. You gave her what she needed for a home, a family, maybe even just being needed, and she gave you what you needed to be the man of the house and provide for a family, to do an honest day's work for an honest day's pay with your hands. You helped raise three great children with dreams and hopes that you supported. You raised them to be honest and truthful and to respect other people. In other words, you invested in the future of mankind. Those three little people will grow up to be brighter, smarter, and better because of what both of you taught them and provided for them. They will take what you and Amanda have given them and share with others who will share with others and so on and so on. From a single acorn grows a mighty oak.

"When you saw Sarah as a nurse while you were with Amanda in the hospital, it was because she had met a doctor who brought out the best in both of them."

"How did you know all that? How could you possible know all that ... unless ... you're not really a doctor ... are you?" I said as my voice trailed off.

We were at the end of the hallway when Doc said, "I have to check on a patient. Let's go in here." We walked in an operating room.

When we entered, the room was full of medical devices blinking, beeping, and whirling. There was about six or seven people in medical gowns standing around a table with someone lying on it. They were talking and moving around and adjusting a bunch of machines. As I moved around the room, trying to get a better view of who they were working on, I noticed that dark shadow again in the corner staring at the guy on the table. This time when it saw me it didn't seem scared, just seemed to stare at me.

Doc walked over to me and said, "Okay, any minute there is going to be a bright light that only you can see. You will hear a question that is meant only for you. Answer it truthfully and you can walk into the light. If you do not, that shadow will take you away. I suggest you answer truthfully and from the heart."

"But what about my family?" I said quietly.

"They will be taken care of no matter how you answer."

"I have to know. Like I asked before, you are not a real doctor, are you?"

"I am many things to many people. But my main job is to help travelers get to where they are going safely. Just like I once helped a baby boy cross a river."

"You mean …"

"Yes, I am St. Christopher, the patron saint of travel."

"How do I ever thank you?"

"Just answer truthfully and from the heart. That will be thanks enough."

"I have so many more questions, but I don't know what to ask fir—"

Just then the ceiling opened, and a very bright light shined in. There seemed to be the sound of swirling wind, and then a very beautiful voice asked me a question. I looked at St. Christopher and smiled and answered, "Yes, I do." There was a loud scream from the corner, and the shadow disappeared through the floor.

I looked at St. Christopher one more time and said, "Thank you. Thank you for everything."

"You are most welcome," he said with a smile. And with that I walked into the light, feeling free and relieved. The light disappeared.

*

One of the doctors in the medical gowns said, "That's it. We've done all we can. I'm calling it." He looked up at the clock. "At seventeen hundred hours on August 30, 2012, Mr. William Stanley passed away."

In the days after my passing, it was hard for my family to understand just what had happened that day on the jobsite. But as time went on, I watched over them as they moved on with their lives. Tommy got married and had three wonderful children of his own. Brian joined the US Navy and served twenty-four years. He also found himself a wife who sometimes traveled with him and managed to put up with all the rest of his travels. She stayed at home to watch and raise their two children, one son and one daughter. And my little princess married Tony, who turned out to be a great guy. They both went to Yale and graduated with top honors and eventually had children of their own.

My Amanda did not remarry despite the many proposals. But thanks to the kids, she was never lonely or sad for too long.

I heard through the grapevine that we will be together again soon, at which point I will finish this chapter of my book and start a new one ... one with our life together here.

OPERATION DOG WATER

CHAPTER 1

Like every morning, the sun shined through the gap in the curtains in the master bedroom of baby blue and crept up the king-size bed until it shined on Mark's face. He squinted, rolled over for a moment, and then gave in to the day. He got up, washed his face, and got dressed, just like every other day. But this was not like every other day. It was his birthday. He walked into the kitchen and opened the refrigerator door.

"Milk! We need milk," Kathy reminded Mark, not turning around from the sink. "And don't forget, we have to be at Doug's by seven for your birthday party."

"I know, I know. I'll be ready. I'll be *ready!*" he said as he finished looking for something to bring for lunch. "Oh, look, you baked me a cake. That's nice," he said, not trying to be funny.

She spun around and yelled, "What are you doing in there? Get out and don't look!" She threw the dish towel at him.

"But I was just looking for ... oh, never mind," he said like a little kid, closing the door. Kathy went back to the dishes. He picked up the towel, put it over the chair, and said, "By the way, since it's the second Tuesday of the month, we have to spend the afternoon in a safety meeting, but I should be home on time." He then changed back to a child's curiosity and enthusiasm: "Whatcha get me?" He smiled as he grabbed a leftover container off the countertop with a silly grin from ear to ear.

Pretending she didn't hear the last comment and looking down in the sink at the dishes, she said in a low voice in an almost-plea, "Please write down the time of the party this time, Mark. Remember what happened last year." She then added, looking up at him, "And if I told you what I got, it wouldn't be a surprise, now would it?"

"Oh all right, be that way. I'll write it down. I've got the pocket notebook you gave me right here." He patted his shirt pocket.

"I know we talked about this before," Kathy said softly. She walked over to the towel, wiped her hands, and then turned to Mark and gently wrapped herself around his arm. "But we really need to get Duke that operation. I hate to see him in so much pain."

"Maybe we should seriously think about … you know," Mark said.

"*What?* I've had him since he was a pup, and he's only ten years old. He still has three or four more good years left. Dr. Todd said he could do the operation right here in town, and Duke would only have to stay there a couple of days. And remember, you said if I came up with half the money, you would pay the other half. Well, I have my half." She was still talking softly, but somehow seem to throw in that little sexy voice that women use when they want something. "Besides, I did promise that if you take care of Duke, I would take care of you." She walked her fingers up the front of his shirt until she got to his chin and softly pinched it.

"How could I refuse anything you say when you talk to me like that?"

She looked up at him seductively and whispered, "You can't."

He kissed her gently on the cheek and said, "I'll write it down right now."

In one smooth movement, he took the pad and pen out of his pocket and wrote down, "Call about Duke's Operation." "There—it's in my visual memory. Anything else?"

Still holding his arm, she whispered in his ear, "Would you please give the dog some water?" and gave him a little nibble on his earlobe.

In a funny Igor voice, he replied, "Yes, Master."

She playfully slapped his arm and let go and started walking to the next room. Over her shoulder, she said, "You're hopeless."

Mark grabbed her by the arm and spun her around, held her close, and said in a low voice, "Yes. Hopelessly in love with you," and kissed her one of those kisses you only see in the movies.

When he pulled back, she gasped and fanned her face with her hand and said, "Why, Rhett Butler, I do declare." There was a brief moment of silence, and then they both broke out into a good laugh.

He let her go, and as she walked away she called out, "Please don't forget about the water for the dog, honey."

"Yes, dear," he said in a low voice. He pulled out his pad again, and wrote just below the note about the dog's operation at the bottom of the page "give the dog water." He put the pad back in his pocket and patted it, a habit he got into to help him remember. It was almost 6:45 a.m. He sat at the table and grabbed a box of cereal and the milk Kathy left out for him.

As he reached for the bowl, Duke came slowly over, sat down, and rested his head on Mark's lap. "What? You too?" He scratched him behind the ear and said, "Let me finish my birthday breakfast, and then it will be your turn. Good boy."

CHAPTER 2

As a boy, Mark and his family lived in the countryside of western Pennsylvania. Growing up in a small town in the late 1970s, life was good and farmland was as far as the eye could see and then some. A ride to the store in their 1968 Ford Torino station wagon would sometimes take an hour or longer, especially if you got stuck behind Mr. Johnson's John Deere tractor. Sometimes it would take forever, like the day of Mark's tenth birthday.

"I'll tell you what," Mark's dad, Martin, said that spring before his October birthday. "You can have that new Schwinn bicycle in Mr. Howard's store window if you can show me that you are ready for the responsibility of having something as important as a bicycle. If you work hard this summer and save your money, I'll put up half of what it costs. Deal?" He put out his hand.

Mark's face lit up, and he shook his dad's hand and said with as much enthusiasm a boy of almost ten could, "*Deal!*"

That whole summer Mark cut grass, trimmed hedges, swept, raked, cleaned garages, and even walked Mrs. Strickland's St. Bernard that was almost as big as he was. He even sometimes helped his friend Ricky with his newspaper route.

As he was walking up the Peterson's driveway, which seemed to be almost a quarter mile long, he thought, *This will be so much easier when I get that bike. Why, I'll bet I could do the whole route myself in half the time Ricky can do it.* Then he pictured himself riding as fast as the wind and racing from one house to the next. The people would come out of their houses to see how fast he could deliver the newspapers. He could see them lining the road and cheering for him as he came flying by. At the end of the street, the high school band would be playing the victory song. The people would throw confetti and be yelling and blowing their car horns …

Yelling? Car horns? *"Look out!"*

Look out? He came out of his daydream only to see the grill of Mr. Peterson's car right in front of him. "Mark, do you mind if I get up my driveway?"

"I'm … I'm sorry, Mr. Peterson. I was just … umm … thinking … uh … of … my new bike. I'm saving up for one for my birthday. I guess I got a little carried away," he said with his voice trailing off as he looked down at the ground.

"Well, I hope you pay more attention to the road when you get it than you do when you are walking."

Mark quickly looked up and said, "Yes, Mr. Peterson, I will, sir."

"Have a nice day, Mark."

Mark stepped onto the grass as Mr. Peterson continued up his driveway.

"Thank you, sir. You too," Mark yelled as he turned and continued down the driveway.

Well, a week before his birthday, after raking Mrs. Nelson's yard, Mrs. Nelson paid him and then offered him a drink. Mark said, "Yes, please, ma'am," and she went back inside to get it.

He was counting his money when Mrs. Nelson came back out the front door, handed him a drink of freshly squeezed lemonade, and said, "Oh, Mark, you did a really good job on the yard, thank you. Oh, dear, I almost forgot."

She went back inside just as Mark started to drink his lemonade. She was gone for just a moment and came back out before the screen door could slam shut.

"I want to give you your birthday present a little early." She handed him an envelope with his name on it.

Mark stopped drinking and smiled. He handed her the glass and thanked her again. He started to walk home, got to the end of the driveway, turned around and waved to her, and then turned around again.

He opened the envelope and pulled out a card that said "Happy Birthday, Big Guy" with a cartoon picture of a giant climbing a beanstalk. When he opened the card, a ten-dollar bill fell out and floated down. It stopped him in his tracks. He watched as it fluttered like a big, green butterfly. He stared at it for a moment and then slowly picked it up. A brand-new ten-dollar bill—no rips, no creases, no wrinkles. He stared at the intense color as he ran his finger over it and felt all the raised print.

He turned around and saw Mrs. Nelson still standing on her porch. He waved frantically and yelled, "Thanks a lot!" He turned and ran the rest of the way home. He ran straight to his room to count all of his money. He smiled from ear to ear when he found out he had half the money for the bike. He was going to have his first brand-new bicycle. He knew his mom would never let him ride it to school.

After all, they did live in the country and the school was fifteen miles away. But he would have enough stories to tell all his friends about the adventures that he will have had … just him and his bike.

As it worked out, his birthday fell on a Saturday that year. Mark was up at the crack of dawn. He was dressed and ready in a flash. He tried to relax waiting for his dad, but his feet wouldn't let him. He tried to watch cartoons, but they seemed to be moving slower than normal. He went in and woke up his little brother, Jake, but even he was being uncooperative. He woke up his little sister, Marie, but she started to cry, and it took him ten whole minutes to get her to stop. He was pacing in the kitchen when his dad finally came in.

"Oh boy! Can we go now, Dad?"

His dad looked up at the clock that was shaped like a chicken on the kitchen wall above the sink and said, "It's only seven thirty! Mr. Howard's store doesn't open until ten on Saturdays."

Suddenly Mark didn't feel like pacing the floor anymore or watching cartoons or bothering his brother or sister. He just stared at his dad for a long minute and said in a faint voice, "I'm going back to bed."

"Happy birthday, son," his dad said softly as he rubbed Mark's head as he walked past.

Mark gave him a half smile and half a hand wave with slouched shoulders and mumbled, "Thanks." He walked slowly back to his room where his brother was still sleeping.

At nine his dad knocked on his door, opened it, and said, "I've got to stop by the bank before we pick out your bike. Want to go now?"

Mark, who was just lying there not able to fall back to sleep, was up with a jump.

His dad had to take a step backward to prevent himself from being run over.

Mark was out the front door before you could say "birthday boy." He ran all the way over to the station wagon and opened the back door to get in like normal.

"Hold on there, sport!" his dad yelled, just getting out the front door of the house. Mark looked back in puzzlement. "You can ride up front. It's just you and me."

It started slowly, but that smile finally reached from ear to ear. The front seat was only for the adults. Even if it was just Dad or Mom driving, the kids had to ride in the back. Mark closed the back door, waited for his dad to catch up, and gave him a hug.

His dad opened the front passenger door and said in a butler-type voice, "After you, sir."

"Why, thank you, James," Mark said as he gave a half bow.

"Get in the car, you clown," his dad said and gave Mark a tap on the back of his head. They both had a good laugh at each other's performance.

As they started out the driveway, Mark was putting on his seatbelt when he looked back at the house and saw his mom, Jeanette, waving from the bedroom window. He waved back and pointed at the front seat to make sure she saw where he was sitting. She clapped her hands in approval. Mark waved once more and then turned straight in his seat to look out the windshield.

They got to the end of the driveway, and Martin put on the turn signal and made a left toward town.

About a mile down the road, Mark asked, "What time is it, Dad?"

"Five minutes later than the last time you asked me," he said with half a smile.

"Why does time go soooo sloowwwly when you don't want it to and so fast when it's like summer vacation?" Mark asked, a little frustrated.

"Time is what you make of it, son. Time teaches us to be patient. Time teaches us to make the most of each moment and not waste it. We are only on this earth for a relatively short time. We not only need to learn patience with ourselves and our abilities, but we need to learn how to get along with each other. If you don't get along with others, it could make time seem like it's slowing down. And, like when you're with your friends, time seems to go fast. It is important to get along with the people around you, do you understand?"

Mark thought about it for a long moment and said, "Yeah, I think so. I shouldn't pick on my brother or sister and I should clean my room up more often, right?"

"Wise beyond your years, my boy, wise beyond your years."

They broke out into another laughing frenzy that lasted for a couple of minutes.

Martin turned on the radio to the "easy listening" station.

Mark started to daydream about his bike and the adventures he was going to have, and then he realized they were entering downtown. They drove up to the first of two traffic lights that the town hosted and made a right onto Davis Drive. They drove past Mr. Howard's Bike Shop and made the second left onto Maple Street, then down one block to the First State Savings and Loan. Martin pulled into the driveway and parked near the front door.

"Do you want to come in or stay ..."

But before he could finish, Mark's door was open and he was jumping out.

As Martin was opening his own door, he felt he should finish the sentence. "Or stay here? I'll only be a minute."

"What, Dad?"

"Nothing, son, nothing at all."

As Martin was closing the driver's door, Mark was already at the bank's front door and was opening it. As his dad got closer, Mark said in a mocking voice of a butler, "After you, sir."

"Thank you, James," his dad said and took a couple of quick steps to avoid Mark's hand, already in flight. But Martin stepped a little too lively, though. His momentum carried him into the next set of glass doors, which he pushed right into ... Mr. Peterson.

Martin, now a little embarrassed, opened the door for Mr. Peterson and said, "I'm sorry, Jack."

"That's okay," he said. And he mumbled, looking down at Mark and remembering their talk on his driveway about Mark saving for a new bike, "Now I see where your son gets his daydreaming from."

"Gets what?" Martin asked.

Mark, sensing Mr. Peterson was going to spill the beans, quickly said, "Let me get that door for you, sir. Have a nice day, Mr. Peterson."

"Thank you, Mark," and he was out the door.

Martin asked, "What was he talking about, Mark?"

"Money, Dad, remember? That is why we are here, right?"

Martin looked at him for a moment, then at Mr. Peterson walking away, back at Mark, shrugged and then said, "Let's go get your bike."

The bank was almost empty this time of the morning, so it didn't take long for them to get to the counter and get the money. They were back at the car in no time. Mark started to tell his dad about the adventures that he wanted to take on his new bike when he heard yelling coming from across the road. It was Joey, a high school dropout, heading fast on a one-way road to nowhere. It seemed to Mark that Joey and his girlfriend weren't getting along so well at that moment, so he stopped paying attention to them and opened his door and continued his story as they started out of the parking lot.

Before he could finish his story, they were pulling into the bike shop's parking lot. Mark looked up and saw the Mr. Howard's Bicycles sign and forgot what he was talking about and jumped out of the car just as his dad was stopping.

He jumped the steps quickly and was almost to the front door when his dad opened his door and said, "Mark ... Mark wait a min—" He didn't get a chance to finish when Mark tried the door.

"It's locked!" Mark yelled in frustration.

"It's only 9:50, buddy. We still have ten minutes. Would you like to get something to drink?" Martin asked, trying to break some of the tension.

"Yeah, I guess so." Mark said as he turned back around to walk down the steps. Letting the full weight of his body fall on each of the steps, he walked back to the car. The sound he made reminded Martin of an old Frankenstein movie.

It was about twenty feet or so to cross the parking lot to the road, and there was a 7-11 across the street. Martin closed his door and said, "Come on, we only have to wait ten minutes. You've waited this long. Can't you wait ten— no—nine more minutes?"

"I guess so," Mark said, still staring at the ground.

Mark walked around to his dad's side of the car, and Martin put his arm around Mark's shoulders and said, "Come on, tell me more about these adventures you and your bike are gonna have."

Mark talked slowly, but as he imagined the adventures, he started to talk a little quicker. When they reached the roadside, his dad said, "Oh, wait here, I forgot my wallet in the front seat."

He trotted back to the car. Mark was becoming more and more caught up in his daydream that he didn't see the pickup truck coming around the corner from Maple Street.

Mark already thought Joey was having a rough morning. But Mark didn't know Joey got into a fight the night before with his dad about the "responsibilities" of driving the pickup, like keeping it clean and gassed up because, after all, the truck still belonged to Joey's dad. Mark didn't know Joey took the truck early Saturday morning without permission to sneak over to see his girlfriend and then got into a fight with her over "what was more important, that truck or her." Mark also didn't know that Joey was in a hurry to get home before his dad found the truck gone. And Mark didn't know that the radio station in Joey's truck was drifting out of range and that Joey was paying more attention to finding a station than to the driving. Time as Mark knew it slowed down.

Martin was reaching for the car door handle; Mark was daydreaming about his bike as he stepped onto the road; and Joey was thinking about his girlfriend and trying to find a clear radio station.

Martin suddenly became aware of his own breathing. In and out. It almost seemed to be getting louder. In and out. It had a type of echo, like in the movies. In and out. He grabbed the door handle. In and out. The sound of the metal handle seemed to multiply, as if there were many metal door handles being opened at once. In and out. From the corner of his eye, he saw the movement of the truck. In and out. He turned to see Mark slowly walking across the street, looking up, lost in his daydream. In and out. He saw the truck, he saw Mark. In and out. The squealing of the tires. In and in and in.

Martin yelled as loud as he could. *"Mark!"*

CHAPTER 3

"Mr. and Mrs. Redwood?" a voice called into the almost-empty waiting area.

"That's us," Martin replied as he stood up from his seat next to Jeanette.

The doctor walked over to them and stuck out his hand and said, "Hi, my name is Dr. Jerry, and I am your son's doctor. First, your son is okay. He took a pretty good bump there, but let me assure you, he'll be just fine. Second, since he took a hit to the head, he could be suffering from a subdural hematoma, a condition that is common with head injuries. I'd like to keep him a few days to run some tests if that's okay with you. Do you have any questions?"

"When can we see him?" Jeanette asked.

"Right now if you'd like, but try not to let him talk too much. We've given him a sedative, and he needs to rest."

"Thank you, Doctor. Thank you very much," Martin said as he stuck his hand out and shook the doctor's hand again.

"If you have any questions, you can reach me here at the hospital. The nurse will contact me any time of the day. I'll keep you informed. Now, go on and see your son."

Dr. Jerry took a step to the side and let Martin and Jeanette go to Mark's room.

They entered the room as quietly as possible, their emotions hidden as well as possible. In all the movies and in all the books, there is nothing that can prepare you to see a loved one in real life in a hospital bed, with IVs, tubes, and wires hooked up to him or her.

Next to the bed was the heart monitor that all the tubes and wires fed into, and it made a beeping sound every five seconds or so. As Jeanette looked around, she noticed Mark was the only one in the small two-patient room. A window on the far wall overlooked a stream and a meadow and a baseball field to the right, where the sound of two local T-ball teams were hitting it out almost out of hearing range. The window was open, and a slight breeze blew just enough to make the curtains flutter. There was also a smell of fresh-cut grass drifting in on the breeze.

Just on the other side of Mark's bed, under the heart monitor, was a nightstand with a lamp on it and a note pad and pencil. There were two chairs in the room, one by each bed. Martin helped Jeanette sit in the one next to Mark's bed. He then picked up the other chair, walked back as quietly as he could, placed it next to Jeanette, and sat. The sun was beginning to set, and it made the room glow. Martin felt like this was all just a dream and he was going to wake up any minute.

Mark was under a white sheet, but the glow from the sun made it seem like gold. His breathing was shallow, and it almost seemed like he had passed away in his sleep. Martin could see that this made Jeanette feel very uneasy, so he took her hand in both of his. As his parents stared at him, remembering the events of the day, from when he waved good-bye from the front seat of the car to when Martin came home to take her to the hospital, they saw Mark's finger move. At first they thought they imagined it. A few seconds later Mark's eye twitched, and his heart monitor beeped faster.

Both Jeanette and Martin started to get up from their chairs when Mark open his eyes and moaned, "Where am I?"

Chapter 4

M ark stayed in the hospital for a week and then had to go back to see the doctor every week for a little more than a month. It was almost Thanksgiving before he went back to school. It was his first week back that he noticed a change in his study habits. He would read something and realize he didn't remember what he had just read. He told the teacher he was having trouble with the assignments, and they told him it would be okay, it was just that he was getting over the shock of the accident and that all he needed was time.

Thanksgiving came and went, and still Mark was struggling with his homework and paying attention in class. When they went back to the doctor for Mark's checkup in December, Dr. Jerry asked if everything was all right and if there were any problems he should know about.

At first Mark sat quietly on the exam table, but then he said as he looked down at his swinging feet, "I can't remember things." There was silence, and then he took a deep breath and continued. "I read things and can't remember what I just read. Or Mom will tell me to do things, and on my way to do them, I forget and have to go back and ask what she wanted me to do. It's driving me crazy, and driving my mom and dad out of their minds. I feel like a failure."

Dr. Jerry thought for a moment and then said, "It's not your fault. I mean that. These things happen to good people all the time, and this time … well … this time it happened to you. But I want you to remember that it isn't your fault. Once you convince yourself of that, you will start to do better, no matter what it is you want to do. Now, repeat after me: 'It was not my fault.'"

Mark mumbled the sentence.

Dr. Jerry said, "Okay, sit up straight and take a deep breath." Mark did. "Good, good. Now repeat after me, 'It was not my fault.'"

This time Mark was a little louder. "It was not my fault."

"Better. One more time, and say it like you mean it."

"It was not my fault." This time Mark sounded like he meant it. Now Mark smiled, as if a great weight had been lifted from his shoulders. It was the first time he had smiled in more than a month.

Dr. Jerry was happy to see Mark smile and said, "Now, what you need to do is to start writing down the things you are having trouble remembering. It will take a little time to get used to, but just like everything else, you will be writing things down without even thinking about them. We can call it your 'visual memory,' a thought or memory you can see in a book or from a pad. It'll become second nature. Do you know what I mean?"

"Yeah, I think so. If I do it enough times, it will be automatic, like when you watch the baseball or football game and you grab the bag of potato chips or pretzels and eat them until they're gone and wonder what happened to the full bag you opened."

"Yes, I think you understand. Now go home and practice writing in your visual memory, and I'll see you next time."

CHAPTER 5

B ack at the breakfast table, after eating his cereal and reading a few articles in the paper, Mark pulled out his notepad and remembered about giving the dog some water. He folded the newspaper and left it on the table, went to the sink, filled a cup with water, and poured it into Duke's bowl, where the dog was waiting patiently. Mark patted him on the head, grabbed his hat and lunch, and went out the door.

No sooner did he get out the front door than Doug yelled over the hedge, "It's about time! I was just coming over to see if you got lost or something." They walked to the sidewalk.

"No, just writing down the day's 'honey-do' list."

"Kathy had a few more things for ya, did she?"

"Yeah, this time it was about the dog."

"Again with the dog? Didn't you put that thing to sleep yet?"

"Shhh, not so loud. You know she can hear through walls."

"Oh, for Pete's sake, let's go," Doug said as he started to walk a little faster.

At the bus stop, they waited to catch the bus for the metro. Just after they got on the train, Mark heard a familiar voice call him from the back. At first he didn't pay any attention because he thought he imagined it. But it got louder. Then someone walked up and sat behind him and said in a stronger voice, "I guess you'd better write down your name so you'll remember it when someone calls you."

"Brian?" Mark said loudly as he turned around. "*Brian!*"

"You scared me there for a moment. I didn't know what I was going to say if you didn't remember me."

"What are you doing here?" Mark asked with a smile.

"I was here on some … business, I guess you could say. My company is expanding, and I had a meeting downtown with some prospects that will finish up today."

Turning toward Doug, who was seated across the aisle, Mark shook his head and said, "I'm sorry, Doug. This is one of best friends from school, Brian DeWalter." Then, turning toward Brian, he said, "Brian, this is one of my best friends from … well … now. Doug Gold."

"Hi, how do you do?" Doug said as he stuck out his hand.

"Any friend of Mark's is a friend of mine," Brian said as he shook Doug's hand. He then pulled him a little closer and said, "Do you have to keep him out of trouble like I did?"

"We'll have to get together and compare notes sometime," Doug said with a half smile.

"Okay, that's enough," Mark said as everyone laughed.

Brian looked at Mark but said to Doug, "There was this one time—"

"Come on, you just met the guy," Mark wined.

"You did say he was your best friend, didn't you?" Brian said to Mark.

"Fine, go ahead."

Brian continued as though he was reliving the moment. "There was this kid named Tommy ... Tommy, something ... Tommy ... Thorton, that's it—he was the class bully. He picked on *everyone*—well, except me because we were the same size. He once pulled one of his tricks on the janitor. He stole one of the janitor's cigarettes and started a fire in the basement with it. When the firemen found the cause of the fire, the school board let the janitor go. There was supposed to be a witness, but he never talked because Tommy took his dog and told the kid that if he said anything, he would eat his dog and leave little pieces of him in his mailbox for a whole year.

"Now, Tommy liked picking on Mark because he towered over Mark like the Empire State Building. Tommy had been picking on Mark since, what, since the beginning of time it seemed like. Well, for three years, anyway.

"One day, Mark was at his locker between classes when Tommy came running up the hall and grabbed him in front of everyone. He stuffed Mark into the locker and closed the door. All Mark could hear was the roar of laughter from the hallway full of kids who saw what happened. He couldn't even bring himself to call for help. I ran down the hall and opened the locker. All I could say was, 'Are you okay?' Red-faced from anger, Mark said, 'We have to get him back.'

"We made this plan to get Tommy back in the lunch room. It was where Tommy could watch the whole room to find his next victim. Tommy stood with his 'wannabees' (you know, younger kids who wanted to be just like him) and saw Mark walking toward him. Tommy says, 'Well, well, well, if it ain't the little locker boy. What are doing on *my* side of the lunch area?'

129

"Mark smiled at him while I snuck around behind Tommy down the handicap ramp so that Tommy was about three feet above me. Without being noticed, I tied a string from a chair to a paperclip and hooked it on Tommy's shoelace.

"Mark smiled and said, 'Well, I'd rather be in a locker than be as dumb as one.'

"Tommy's face turned red. Mark had turned on one heel and was running for the door. He had a good start before he heard 'freight-train Tommy' with this chair tied to his shoe coming after him. Because Mark was smaller, he was maneuvering around the chairs and tables faster than a church mouse heading to the pancake breakfast. Tommy finally broke the string, and then he was throwing chairs and knocking over tables as he forced his way through the lunch room. The other kids were laughing and cheering as Mark ran for the door. Mark shot through the door and then ran through a door right before the hallway that someone had opened for him.

"Tommy chased after Mark as I ran to the main office to report trouble in the lunchroom. When Mr. Lees, the principal, heard, he headed toward the action. As Tommy ran through the door Mark just had, he was moving too fast and ran straight into Mr. Lees. He hit Lees so hard that both of them fell on the floor and tumbled. A loud gasp came from all the kids in the hallway.

"As Mr. Lees got up, he said in a voice that was heard in three counties, '*To my office—now!*'

"I saw Mark looking out from the room he had jumped into as he was watching Mr. Lees 'helping' Tommy down the hall by the way of his ear. And then Mark turned to thank the person who had opened the door for him. None other than … Kathy."

"So *that's* how you met Miss Wonderful, huh?" Doug asked.

"Yep, and the rest, as they say, is history."

Chapter 6

The metro pulled into the downtown station, and Brian, Mark, and Doug exited the train. They stood there for a minute lost in thought, and then Brian said, "I've got to hit the bathroom before I go any farther. Too much coffee, I guess. I'm only in town for a couple of days on business, but I'm free tomorrow night. Let's do something."

Doug said, "If you've got a couple of hours tonight, we're throwing the birthday boy a party at my house."

Mark turned a little red and added, "It would be pretty great if you could stop by. Kathy will be there, and I'm sure she'd like to see you."

"Okay, okay," Brian said. "Let me see what I can do. How do I get in touch with you?"

"Let me give you my number." Mark pulled out his pad and saw that there were no more blank pages. So he wrote his phone number on the back of the last page, ripped off that corner, and gave it to Brian, saying, "Let's not wait another ten years before we talk again, okay?"

"You got it. Take care, Mark, and it was nice to meet you, Dan."

"*Doug!*" Doug said over the noise of the metro cars pulling out.

"Sorry, *Doug*. Next time I'll take you up on that note thing."

"Great!" Doug said, and they both looked at Mark, who was looking at the sky and shaking his head.

Brian shook their hands and disappeared into the crowd.

"Seems like a nice guy," Doug said.

"Yeah, one of the best. He pulled me out of a few jams in school."

"A few?" Doug asked, looking at Mark sideways.

"You're funny. You should take it on the road. Way down the road." After a moment of silence, they both gave a quick chuckle.

Mark said, "Oh man, it's almost eight. I'm gonna be late. I'll see you for lunch, right?"

"Yeah. The usual?"

"You bet."

As Mark turned to wave at Doug, he tripped over a loose brick in the walkway and dropped his cell phone without noticing. Doug gave a little chuckle at the dance move but didn't see the phone fall either. The phone bounced over to the edge of the platform and fell toward the tracks. It landed under the platform. Mark looked at what he had tripped over and kept walking to the jobsite.

*

While in the bathroom, Brian's cell phone rang. He reached into his pocket and pulled it out, along with the piece of paper with Mark's phone number, but the paper fell to the floor and under the sink. Brian answered his phone and started talking, and as he left the restroom, he never noticed the fallen piece of paper.

CHAPTER 7

Mark was able to check in before the eight o'clock whistle.

His crew leader was standing by the entrance to the jobsite, staring at his watch. "Cutting it pretty close, aren't we, Mr. Redwood?"

"Close, yes. Late? No. There is a difference, Chief," Mark said to the retired Chief Steelworker.

Chief Bowmen was a twenty-five-year veteran of the US Navy Seabees. Even though he retired almost ten years ago, he sometimes thought he was still in. Those who served in the military understood. Those who were not, tolerated him because there really wasn't anybody else you would want on your side in an office argument or a jobsite brawl. He was fair to everyone on his crew, veteran or not. He had a job to do and he was going to get it done, one way or another.

"Grab your belt and get to the fourth deck and help Anderson with those two-by-fours."

"Aye-aye, Chief," Mark said with smile and a sloppy two-finger salute.

"Stow that chatter and move out."

Mark got his belt and was on the fourth floor of the new downtown Hilton helping Joe Anderson staging two-by-fours into the future business lounge while listening to the local rock station. After a while, a 38 Special song came on.

Joe said, "I haven't heard this song in a long time. Turn it up, Mark."

"It's ten to nine in the morning. Do you really want to wind Chief up so early?" Mark asked, looking over his shoulder at Joe.

"What's the dif? We do it now or later."

Mark turn up the volume. He said, "Just remember, the last time you asked me to turn up the radio, the station faded out and that rap station came in clear. Chief was up here in two seconds."

"You know ..." Joe said, "it was a good song in its day. And besides, we don't need to get Chief all wound up so early."

Mark lowered the volume and said, "Good thinking."

Just then, Chief came up on deck and yelled, "I've told you guys to keep that radio low until midday. Now what's all the noise?"

"I ... I ... I'm sorry, Chief," Joe stammered.

"This is your last warning. Next time I toss that noisemaker over the side. Got it?"

Mark and Joe said together, "Got it, Chief."

"Get back to it then. You're burning up my daylight." Chief left the floor.

Joe turned to Mark and said, "Thanks for turning up the radio, Maestro."

Mark looked at Joe with surprise and said, "Maybe I'll just take Chief's suggestion and throw it overboard myself!"

Joe was going to say something in retaliation, but he had other things on his mind. His face softened and he said, "Hey, Mark? I was watching the news last night and they had some top 'expert' on the subject of terrorist attacks and how they could be here now, waiting for some kind of sign to do us all in. He said the FBI was able to deter an attack just a couple of weeks ago. Do you think they're going to try again?"

Mark thought for a moment. Could it happen again? He thought that it was possible. But *would* it? He didn't think so because the country had learned a lot from what had happened over the years. Joe took the New York attack pretty hard and worried uncontrollably for weeks after, even to a point where he almost didn't come out of his house for a week. He then realized that was no way to live, running and hiding from these terrorists. So he pulled himself together and did what everyone else across the states did: he got on with his life.

So Mark tried to answer him without trying to bring all those fears back and said, "Not in our lifetime. Our government learned a lot from all those events. They won't let it happen again."

"Yeah … yeah, you're right. Not in our lifetime," Joe said, half-believing it. "So what now?"

Mark was walking toward the radio. He looked back over his shoulder and said, "Just like the Chief said, turn down the radio and get back to work. We do what we can, and then we move on. Got it?" Mark thought it sounded kind of harsh but decided to just leave it alone.

"Right. Let's finish stacking these two-by-fours," Joe said, feeling a little better.

Chapter 8

H enry Strange. Sheriff Henry Strange. The kind of guy
you only read about in fiction books. Oh, he knows
the law all right, but he lacks—shall we say *tact*—when it
comes to it. He did five years in the army, where he was an
MP and got the bug for law enforcement real bad. He used
to hang out at the club in his uniform and wait for a fight
to break out just so he could be the first on the scene and
make the bust. Some say he used to pay some of the lower
ranks to start a fight and let them slide out the back when he
made the bust. He learned really fast where to be and where
not to be, like right in the middle of it when it started. He
learned to wait for a bust until the fight was going real good,
and that way he could get more people involved.

He got out of the army and joined the police force, but
after a year of trying, they told him he wasn't what they
were looking for. But he did find a job with the sheriff's
department. It wasn't the fast pace he wanted or what he
was looking for, but it was a start, and the town really
needed someone to fill the position. After eight years of
working his way up the ladder to sheriff (since the last
sheriff had to retire at age seventy-six and Henry was the
only deputy), he now wanted to be an FBI agent. After all,
that was where all the action was, right? He felt that all he

needed was one big break, one big case to solve and that would make the FBI come around and see he was agent material. One big case—and he was willing to do almost anything to get it. Not to mention he was running out of time before he would be too old to be an agent. The cut off age was thirty-four.

It was just after nine a.m., and the sheriff was sitting at his desk with his feet up on the corner when he opened the paper and mumbled, "Nothing ever happens around here. It always happens somewhere else. Same thing, different day. I need to get to the city, where things are happening every day. I'm dying up here."

His deputy, who was sweeping out the empty jail cells, said, "You just need some music to calm yourself down. Here, allow me." He walked over to the radio on the sheriff's desk and turned it on.

The sound of Mozart's soft, calming classical music filled the office. "There, feel better, Sheriff?"

The sheriff smiled and said, "You know, that is kind of—"

"Beep ... beep ... beep ..." blared the radio station.

"*Oh no!*" the sheriff shouted. "We must be under attack!"

"A car bomb went off just moments ago in the town of Rockwood, Pennsylvania. The car believed to be a Toyota Celica was parked just outside the Union Bank. Amazingly, only one person was killed in the blast and five injured. Stay tuned for more up-to-the-minute reports on this incident."

Sheriff Strange jumped to his feet in one swift movement and yelled as loud as he could, "Holy terrorist act, Batman! That's only about an hour away from here. I need to be there. They *need me!*" He turned off the radio and grabbed the phone and hit number two on his speed dial. "Hello, Commissioner? Did you hear what's going on in Rockwood? They're going to need all the help they can get. I want to volunteer. I can be packed and ready to go in ten minutes. All I need is your go-ahead."

"Yes, Sheriff, we just heard the news also. Frankly, I was wondering how long it would take you to call. Even though I know they are in a world of hurt right now, the fallout from this is going to be pretty big, considering that some of us have relatives in that area. That's why I've decided to have you stay here."

"Thank you, Commissioner. I'll make you proud. When I get interviewed, I'll make sure I'll mention your name and how you said … wait … did you say *stay here?*"

"Yes, *stay here.* There are going to be a lot of people depending on you more than ever now to make them feel safe. There has been a possible terrorist act committed here, in our own state, on our own soil. People are going to be scared; they are going to be counting on *you* to protect them. I'm afraid I cannot let you go and leave everything to your deputy. What if we're next? We need you now more than ever, Sheriff."

With a feeling like he'd just lost the big game to a rival high school, the sheriff let out a heavy sigh, and said, "You're … You're right, Commissioner. I shouldn't leave things to chance. I'll take care of this town like I swore I would when I took office. I won't let you or the town down, not now, not in this time of need. I'll protect this town if it's the last thing I do."

"Yes, yes, I'm sure you will, Sheriff Strange. I'm sure you will. Keep me posted. I'm calling an emergency town meeting for tonight. I'll talk to you then."

"Yes, sir," Sheriff Strange said and hung up. He stood there for a moment, pulled up his pants, and said in a loud and low voice, "Deputy, we have work to do."

CHAPTER 9

The young deputy, Miles Frederickson, did not seem like the sharpest pencil in the box. He was good at doing what he was told: cleaning the cells, typing reports, and taking out the trash. Sometimes he was even trusted with going to KFC for the sheriff's meals. But anything more than that at times would appear to be, shall we say, pushing it. His grandfather was a sheriff, his uncles were all sheriffs at one time or another, and his dad was the sheriff three towns away. So, to him, his future was clear. Someday he would be sheriff, and when he found his one true love, his sons would someday be the sheriff.

Miles was the kid everyone picked on growing up. Even the geeks picked on him. He received good grades (not great but good). He was kind of a klutz. Walking around with his shoes untied, he'd often trip and drop all his books. The other kids were afraid to be with him in gym class or in the lunch room because they didn't want to get hurt when he would have one of his moments. One year for a science project he made an active volcano. He spent weeks on it. With no help from his mom or dad, he made this volcano with a motor in the base and a timing device so when you pushed the button, the board that the volcano sat on would vibrate and smoke would come out the top. He tested it, he brought it in for a grade, and it worked three or four times.

The night of the science fair, as the judges were at his table, he was explaining how a volcano works, but when he pushed the button nothing happened because he forgot to plug it in. So he climbed under the table, and when he plugged in the extension cord, he heard a loud bang and then yelling. When he came out from under the table, he had to wave his hand back and forth to help clear the smoke and saw everyone that was standing around his table was covered with papier-mâché and ketchup, which he added to look like lava for effect for when the volcano erupted.

No one was sure what went wrong, but as the judges were walking away, one of them said, "Only you, Miles, only you." Even to this day, someone would see Miles on the street, grocery store, or gas station and yell, "Hey, Volcano Boy!" It was tough growing up in a small town. People don't forget.

But other than growing up rough, Miles was a good guy to talk to. He'd listen to anyone who just wanted to talk. And, like I said, he did what he was told. That's why Sheriff Strange liked having him around.

"Deputy, I need you pull out the town's evacuation plans and update them for tonight's emergency meeting. Then I want you to make up some signs to inform everyone about the meeting and get one to all the stores in town and maybe put some up on the telephone poles. Get your two brothers to help. Tell them I will pay them for the day's work, if they can fit it into their busy schedule. I really wish you could be more like them. Sometimes I don't know why I keep you around. Why can't you be more like your brothers?"

Under his breath, Miles said, "Maybe because no one else will work with you?"

Turning his head sharply and squinting, the sheriff bellowed, "What? What was that?"

"Nothing. I just said maybe they're at work, and I would try them here."

"Oh, yeah, okay. Now you're thinking. Stick with me, kid, and you'll go far."

CHAPTER 10

Every day around noon, Chief grabbed his bullhorn and let out three long beeps for lunch break. Mark and Joe climbed down from the fourth floor on the ladders because everyone else was using the elevator.

When Mark got down to the ground and was almost out the gate, he reached for his phone, but it wasn't in his pocket. He remembered putting it in his jacket, and then he remembered his jacket was on the fourth floor. Joe told him to forget about it, it will still be there when they got back.

"But I was going to call Kathy and ask if she needed anything from the store," Mark replied.

"You can use mine. We're gonna be the last ones in line, and then we'll be late coming back. Come on."

Mark agreed and they left for lunch.

About two blocks down the road, they ran into Doug, who was going to lunch. "Hey, Doug. How's it going at work?" Mark asked.

"Don't ask," Doug said in a low voice. "What a morning. Did you guys hear what happened in Rockwood this morning? Our phones haven't stopped ringing."

Joe said, "No, what happened?"

Mark jumped behind Joe and moved his hand back and forth across his throat, meaning don't say anything.

"Oh ... umm ... the ... the ... cat! Yeah, the cat. It seems that some ... body in the ... umm ... mayor's ... office ... umm ... yeah, this guy, who works in the mayor's office, he, umm, he ran over this, this cat, you see ... in front of ... umm ... yeah, in front of a bunch of kids. Yeah, they ... they all took it real hard. And now, the, umm, animal control people are ... are really up in arms about this. This thing."

Joe turned around and looked at Mark, who turned quickly and was looking across the street.

Joe looked back at Doug and said, "I don't believe it."

Mark looked up in the air and rolled his eyes. Doug was about to apologize when Joe cut in and said, "Those ... those government guys think they can get away with anything. Ran over a cat in front of a bunch of kids? I'll bet some of them will need therapy, and you know who's gonna pay for it? You bet. You and me out of our tax dollars. When I get home tonight, I'm writing an e-mail to that mayor and have him make *that* guy pay for the therapy. That'll teach him." With that, he walked past Doug like a man on a mission and continued to go to lunch.

Doug looked at Mark and whispered, "What was that all about?"

Mark waved his hand back and forth and said, "Don't ask. I'll tell you tonight. It'll sound better after a few beers." They started to follow Joe, and then Mark said, "Hey, you got your phone? I have to call Kathy."

Still a little puzzled and watching Joe as he walked in front of them, Doug said, "Yeah, sure. Here you go," and handed Mark his cell phone.

*

Across town, Sheriff Strange was having a fit. "Why won't they do something? Are they just going to let these foreigners just come here to our home and blow it all apart, one town at a time? What kind of government do we have here anyway?"

"Now, Sheriff," his deputy cut in. "I'm sure our government is doing the best they can, under the circumstances. They'll get them boys, one way or another. You just have to believe that our system works."

"Step down off your soapbox now, Deputy. Did you get started on those fliers yet, like I told you?"

"All done, Sheriff."

"*All done?* How can you be *all done* when it takes you half a day to do a daily report?"

"I finally got my laptop fixed. You see, in attempting to flash your basic input-output system, it was receiving an error 144, and as the directory is not sub to the root directory; the battery cannot be identified as hardware. This is a common fault, but all it needed was a fresh AC adaptor in order to proceed with the BIOS flash. That's why I wasn't able to get those reports done as fast as I should. Now that I fixed my computer, I don't have to use yours, which is still running at a rate of approximately 8 MHz with RAM capacity of 256 kb."

Sheriff Strange just stood there for a long minute with a dumbfounded look of disbelief in what he just heard.

"Did I say something wrong, Sheriff?" Miles asked as he waved his hand up and down in front of the sheriff's face.

He finally came out of whatever trance he was in and yelled, "Get your paws away from my face, Deputy. We have work to do. We have to make sure this town is secure."

CHAPTER 11

The sheriff and the deputy started down Main Street. As they walked and stapled posters up on the telephone poles, the deputy kept asking questions about what they were going to do next and how they would proceed. He asked a whole bunch of questions on how to handle the prisoners, if they caught anyone.

The sheriff said, "You sure ask a lot of questions, dontcha?"

"Knowledge is power. The only dumb question is the one not asked. It is better to ask and not need it—"

The deputy didn't get a chance to finish his sentence when the sheriff waved his hand in front of Miles's face and stopped him in his tracks. "That's enough. Okay, you keep looking around here. I'm going down to the train station. If they can attack our buildings, they could attack our transportation as well. I'll just have a look around. I'll meet you back at the office for lunch." As the sheriff stood there looking out into nowhere land, he stiffened up his lips, squinted his eyes, and pulled up his pants by the belt.

Miles thought he looked like a three-hundred-pound Barney Fife and gave a little chuckle. The sheriff quickly looked at him with his eyes still squinting and said, "What's so funny, Deputy?" with a heavy accent on "deputy."

"I … umm … I … I was just thinking of something I saw on TV just last night. It was an—"

"That boob tube is making your head soft, Deputy. If you want to last in this business, you have to keep your head clear and razor sharp, like mine. Now get moving."

The deputy just smiled and walked off, looking in the store fronts and between cars. The sheriff gave one more tug on his pants and he was off to the train station.

Once the sheriff was at the train station, the few people walking around came up to him and were asking about the car bomb and what he knew about it. He just pushed past them and told them he was on official business and didn't have time to answer so many questions.

As he slowly looked around, walking like he had no direction, he decided to check out the platform. A couple of girls in their early twenties were walking toward him, so he sucked in his gut and tried to look important. Then he smiled and tipped his hat toward them as they walked past. He relaxed and turned to look at them when he grabbed the hand rail for the stairs. Just as he turned his head to look, he stuck his hand in some gum hidden under the rail. He pulled his hand back, lost his balance, and took a step back with a little screech like a little kid. He tried to recover by making a coughing sound, but it was too late.

The girls were laughing and giggling at the funny sound. He started back up the stairs, looking at the rail without using it, and entered the restroom. As he was washing his hands, he complained under his breath about how kids today get away with so much stuff and how he would have liked to catch the little brat who left that piece of gum on the railing. He pulled off a couple of pieces of paper towels, wiped his hands, and looked at the trash can and pretended that he was on a basketball court with hundreds of people watching. He took a step back and said "He's back, he shoots, and ..." He threw the paper towel toward the trash can but missed. Then he added "end of game." He walked over to the trash can, bent over to pick up the towel, and saw another piece of paper on the floor.

"Litter bugs. I hate them ..." His voice tapered off when he saw what was written on it. "What's this? Operation *Dog Water*? What does that mean?" He went to throw it away, but then the wheels starting to turn in his head. "They were here. The terrorists. We *were* the next target. Operation Dog Water. What are they talking about? Let's see, operation—I understand that. Dog ... umm ... could be another word for 'infidel.' Water—think, think. I know ... water supply. Yeah, that's it. They've done something to the water supply. No, that's not it. The car bomb wasn't near the water supply."

Then, with a look like he just discovered the cure for cancer, he yelled, "They are talking about a bomb! Bomb the water supply. That's it! Bomb the water supply. But what water supply?" the sheriff asked as he looked around. "I'm in the restroom. There is a water supply here. The bomb is here in the restroom!"

Just then, one of the stall doors busted open. The sheriff reached for his gun thinking they were on to him. Chris McPhay, an eight-year-old, came running out with one hand on his pants, the other in front of him, and a long piece of toilet paper streaming out of his pants behind him. Once the kid got to the door, he screamed so loud the sheriff thought maybe he did let off a shot after all.

When the sheriff calmed down enough, he got back to the note. He turned it over and saw the phone number. "The contact number? That's what this has got to be. I've got to call the FBI on this. They are gonna want to see this." So he pulled out his cell phone and hit the number on his quick list (you know, just in case he should ever need it), but quickly hung up. Her considered his options. *If they come in now, I'll have to give them everything. I won't get credit for nothing. No, no way. I'll collect all I can and then call them. Then they'll see I'm the guy they need at the FBI.*

Sheriff Strange then went into a daydream with himself in a convertible going down Main Street with confetti falling from the sky and people cheering and the band playing. They pull up to the center of town where the mayor is giving a thank-you speech to their very own hero, Sheriff Strange. Just as the mayor is handing the "key to the city" to the sheriff, a little voice calls out, "Hey, Sheriff, is there really a bomb in here?"

Sheriff Strange snapped out of his daydream to see ten-year-old Bobby Dickinson in front of him.

"Are you okay?" Bobby asked with a look of confusion.

"Fine, just fine. What are you doing in here? Out, out, *out*! I'm closing this place down," the sheriff said in a low voice. "I've got work to do."

CHAPTER 12

Everyone made it back from lunch on time and they all gathered for the training afternoon. Chief got a call that the instructor was running late, so around one o'clock he sent everyone through the site for a trash detail to waste time until the instructor got there. Everyone gathered on the first floor of the new building again around one thirty and waited for the instructor another fifteen minutes before Chief got another call saying the instructor got an emergency call and would not be there.

Chief stood in front of everyone and said, "I need a volunteer to do a safety lecture. Joe, thank you for volunteering."

Joe looked around and then pointed to himself. "*Me?* I didn't volunteer."

"Sure you did. Thank you. Now come up here and give us a lecture."

As Joe walked up to the front of the crew, he said, "Well, what's the lecture on?"

Chief handed him a book and said, "I don't know. It's your lecture."

Joe looked at the cover of the book that said *Safety Is Everyone's Responsibility: Safety Lectures for Construction.* Joe looked at Chief a little puzzled.

Chief said "Just pick a topic."

Joe opened the book that listed about a hundred lectures for safety on the job. Then he looked up at everyone standing around and then at Chief, who just pointed to the book and then looked back at it. He closed it, measured about halfway through, and opened it again. Then he said, "Today's safety lecture is on ... umm ... ladders. When using a ladder on a jobsite, it is important to remember a few safety rules."

Joe read the few pages on "ladder safety" and then said, "If you follow these simple rules, your jobsite will be safer because of it. That's it."

Chief said, "Okay, any questions? Good. You all have a nice afternoon, and I'll see you in the morning before zero eight hundred."

That's all it took. All you could hear was a small stampede and the total evacuation of the jobsite.

Then Mark said, "I've got to call Kathy and let her know I'm coming home early." Mark reached for his phone but then remembered he put it in his jacket pocket, which he left on the fourth floor before lunch. He climbed all the way up to the fourth floor and found his jacket, but when he reached into the pocket, the phone was gone. He searched all over the fourth floor, behind and under the two-by-fours that they stacked, and even in the room where the wood was stored. He worked his way down to the main floor where he found Chuck, an electrician, just getting into his truck.

Mark called out, "Hey, Chuck. Let me use your phone real quick. I think I dropped mine somewhere around here."

Chuck said, "I don't think so."

Mark looked at him in surprise. "Why not?"

Chuck said with a half smile, "You didn't use the magic word."

"Please, may I use your cell phone to find mine, pleeeaassee?" Mark said in kind of a whine.

"Since you asked so nicely, sure." Chuck handed him his new cell phone.

Mark dialed his number and started to look around to see if he would be able to hear it. Then Chuck asked, "Hey, Mark, I have an extra Pepsi. You want it?"

Mark smiled and said, "Sure, I'm really thirsty. Oh … umm … thank you very much, sir."

"Smart aleck," Chuck said half to himself as he took a sip of his own soda.

*

As Mark listened into the phone and to the jobsite at the same time, across town his cell phone rang. Now the sheriff was just about to leave the train platform when he heard a phone ring. He turned and noticed there was no one left standing around, so he started toward the ringing coming from the track area. He jumped onto the tracks and the ringing stopped, but he still did not see a phone.

*

Mark heard his voice mail and turned to Chuck and said, "One more time, please." Chuck took another sip of his soda with one hand and waved with his other, meaning go ahead.

Mark hit redial and started walking toward the building to try to hear better for the phone ring.

*

The sheriff was still looking but could not see the phone.

*

As Mark started to hear his phone ring, he took a sip of his Pepsi.

*

When the phone started to ring under the platform, the sheriff saw it, grabbed it, flipped it open, and said, "Hello?"

*

Not expecting to hear someone answer the phone, Mark tried to say something, but all that came out was a kind of gurgle because of the soda. When he did this, he tripped over a rock and dropped the phone, which smashed into pieces.

*

The sheriff's eye's opened wide, and he said, "That sure as hell was not English. That was definitely foreign, maybe Middle Eastern. Hey, wait a minute." He pulled the message out of his pocket and checked the number on the back of the ripped piece of paper, comparing it to the number from the phone under "My Phone Number Is." The sheriff's face lost all blood and now looked pale as a ghost. "They match."

*

Back across town, you could almost hear Chuck yelling in Florida. "What did you do? I just got that thing a couple of days ago."

"I am really sorry, but I tripped over this rock and—wait a minute. Someone answered my phone. That means it's not here. So where is it?

Chapter 13

The sheriff got back to his car, still in a daze, not sure of what he was going to do. "First things first," he said to himself. "I'm going to need some help. I'm going to need a … *task force*. Yeah, yeah. And some help from the big boys too. This is going to put this town on the map. Wait. This is going to put *me* on the map. Maybe they'll change the name of the town to 'Strangeville.'" After saying it out loud, he thought about it and then said, "Ah, maybe 'Henryville.' Yeah, that sounds better."

The sheriff got back to the office and found his deputy sitting at his desk working on the computer. As soon as Strange opened the door, he started barking orders: "Deputy, first I need you to recall a few people for our task force. Call Terri, oh, what's her name to be the scribe, not Ms. Know-it-all Carol. I hate when she interrupts me all the time. Next, I want—"

"We have a *task force*? What's going on, Sheriff?"

"Didn't I *just* say I didn't like being interrupted when *I'm* speaking? Geez, man, just listen for now and I'll explain. Next I am going to need five, no wait, *ten* deputies for back up when we make the bust. You'd better let the doc know we may need him too, just in case things get messy. And you'd better clean up the briefing room so we can start the plotting charts." He stopped and took in a deep breath, looking around the room. His stare darted at the deputy and he yelled, "Well, let's go. Chop, chop. We have work to do."

"But you said you were going to explain, Sheriff. Are we under attack?"

"Better! I got him, I got the guy who was going to bomb *this* town." The sheriff beamed.

The deputy jumped out of his chair and said, "Where is he? Should I go with you and get him out of the car?"

"I don't *have him* have him, per se. But I have his phone and a note he left for … wait a minute …" His voice trailed off. He looked above the door as if the answer was written there. "Who did he leave that note for? Maybe I should have left it there so I could catch them both. Hmm …" He acted like he'd fallen into a dreamlike state.

"Ahh … Sheriff? Are you still with me?" the deputy said, waving his hand in front of the sheriff's face.

"What the … huh … why do you keep doing that?" the sheriff asked, snapping out of his daydream, swatting his hands at the deputy. The sheriff fell back into his trance for a moment and then snapped out of it, yelling, "Get in the car, Deputy. We're going on a stakeout."

CHAPTER 14

Back at the jobsite, Mark and Chuck picked up the all the pieces of the broken phone, and after ten minutes of Chuck complaining, they left the jobsite for the night. Mark still could not imagine who had his phone or what country they were calling to leave him with a huge bill to pay. He decided to look around the jobsite one more time, this time looking for someone with it and wondering why the person would have his phone. After about an hour of looking around, he thought he might stop by the sheriff's office to see if maybe someone had dropped it off. He went to write it down but then thought he would hopefully remember without depending on his visual memory.

On the way, as he was walking through town, he thought about what had happened in Rockwood and about the car bomb and those people who had been injured and killed, and then his stomach made a sound. He thought he would stop by the local Food Mart to pick up a little something before supper. He was passing the sheriff's office just as the sheriff and deputy were coming out the front door.

"Afternoon, Sheriff … Hi, Miles. How are you doing today?" Mark asked.

"Not now, civilian. Just keep moving," the sheriff said as he pulled up his pants by the belt, not really looking at Mark and trying to look important.

The deputy said, "Oh, hey, Mark. How's Kathy doing?" The sheriff lowered his head and looked up at Miles over his mirrored sunglasses and then looked back at the street. Miles looked at the sheriff and felt like he was going to get detention and then looked back at Mark. He said, "Sorry, Mark, can't stop and talk right now, we're on our way to a stakeout. We're going down to the—"

The sheriff sternly looked at the deputy and smacked him with the back of his hand in the middle of the deputy's chest. "Shut your pie hole, would you? Honestly, you're worse than the five o'clock news."

Mark watched the Laurel and Hardy act for a couple of minutes, said to have a good day, and headed for the supermarket. He felt like he was forgetting something but kept walking.

The sheriff watched Mark walk away and said in a low voice, "There's something about him I can't put my finger on. But what is it?"

Mark walked into the supermarket and headed for the frozen-food section. He stopped at a freezer and was just staring into one of the glass doors, thinking of his phone and the voice he'd heard answer it, when someone said, "You have to open the door to get what you want. It won't come out to you."

Mark saw Doug staring at him. "I'm sorry, what?"

"The food. It won't come out to you. You have to ... ahh, never mind. It's not funny if you have to explain it. Are you okay? You seem, I don't know, preoccupied."

"I dropped my phone somewhere, and when I borrowed another phone to find mine someone answered. I was just wondering which country the guy was calling to do me in on the phone bill."

"I think I can help with that," Doug said as he pulled out his phone.

"I don't think—" Mark started to say.

"I know you don't, but I just want to try … shh." Doug waved his hand at Mark. "Shelly, hi, it's Doug. I need you check a number for me." He shared the number with her.

Mark said, "Are you sure you're not going to get into trouble for this?"

"Yes, just trace it and see where it is. Thanks. Yes, I'll wait." He covered the phone and said in a loud whisper, "She is triangulating the signal. We should know somethi—yes, I'm still here. It's *where?*" Doug quickly looked at Mark and said, "It's right outside?"

Mark put down his empty basket and ran for the front door with Doug close at his heels. As they got to the sidewalk, they looked for anyone using a cell phone, but all they saw was the sheriff's car driving away.

CHAPTER 15

In the sheriff's car, the deputy got into the driver's side, fastened his seatbelt, and adjusted the rear-view mirror. He saw Mark and Doug run out of the supermarket but didn't give it another thought. As he was pulling out onto the road, he turned to the sheriff and said, "So are you going to tell me where we're going?"

The sheriff came out of his daydream of him accepting the position of the FBI's deputy director of the entire East Coast, and said, "*What?* Oh, yeah. Umm ... head to the train station. We'll start there."

"The train station?" The deputy took his eyes off the road for a minute to look at the sheriff.

"Yes, the *train station*, that's what I said, didn't I? Just drive, will ya? I'm the *deputy direct*—I mean I'm the sheriff, so just do as you're told, Dep-u-ty." He rolled his eyes.

They drove the rest of the way in silence as it started to get dark. As they pulled up to the train station, the deputy turned off the headlights, drove about twenty feet more, and came to a stop. They had their eyes glued to the station. It was all quiet for about five minutes when they thought they heard a noise coming from the restroom.

The deputy turned to the sheriff and said, "Did you hear that?"

"Shh … just listen."

Just then they saw a shadow moving in the men's restroom window.

Again the deputy said, "Did you—"

"Let's move. We got him!" the sheriff said, opening his door.

The deputy was right behind him.

Using moves one would only see on TV, with their guns drawn, they zigzagged up to the train platform, ducked under the yellow police tape the sheriff put up earlier that day, and stopped just outside the men's restroom. With the sheriff next to the door and the deputy right behind him, the sheriff moved his head to motion his partner to the other side of the door. Not understanding the head move, the deputy squeezed up next to the sheriff, pushing him closer to the door.

The sheriff looked at him nervously, and in a loud whisper said, "What are you doing, you crazy little … just get to the other side of the door, will you?"

"Oh, okay." He moved to the other side, shuffling his feet.

"Shhhhhhh … do you want him to hear you? Some deputy you are." Then he changed his facial expression and said very professionally, "Now, on the count of three, you first. One, two …"

"Why do I have to go first?"

"*Three, go!*"

The deputy pushed open the door and pointed his gun in every direction. After not hearing any shots, the sheriff entered. They moved into the restroom, and when they were by the sinks, they heard a noise in one of the stalls.

The sheriff looked at the deputy and motioned to the stalls. They moved over to the first one and the sheriff mouth the words, "One, two, *three!*" and pushed open the door. Nothing.

They moved over to the next one and again he mouthed, "One, two, *three!*" Again, nothing.

They moved to the next one, and this time, when the sheriff mouthed, "One, two …" the last stall door slammed open.

"*Don't shoot! Don't shoot!*" eight-year-old Chris McPhay screamed—again.

Both the sheriff and deputy fumbled with their guns before they drew a bead on the young boy.

Chris said, "I snuck out of my house to come back to look for my dad's phone I borrowed. I have to find it before he gets home. I thought I dropped it in here this afternoon, when you thought there was a bomb in here."

The deputy said, looking at the sheriff, "There's a *bomb* in here?"

"Not now, Deputy. Wait … *you* dropped the phone?" the sheriff asked.

"Yes, my dad lent it to me and I dropped it somewhere. Have you seen it?"

The sheriff and deputy lowered their guns.

"Come on, let's go downtown and call your dad," the sheriff said with a little disappointment in his voice.

CHAPTER 16

After walking around for about fifteen minutes, Mark said, "I don't see anyone out here. Are you sure she said right outside? Maybe you gave her the wrong number."

"Hey," Doug said, "this isn't my first rodeo. I've done this before. I don't get it … we usually get the person. Let me try again." Doug took the phone out of his pocket, hit redial, and said, "Hi, Shelly, it's me again. Can you try that number again? Thanks, I'll wait." He covered the mouthpiece and said, "Mark, did you call Kathy yet? I'll bet she's getting worried."

"Ah, man. I completely forgot. She's gonna kill me."

"You can use my phone … oh, wait … yes … yes, Shelly, I'm still here. Oh, really. Thanks a lot. I owe you one. What's that? Oh, okay, I owe you two." He looked at Mark with a kind of confused look and said, "Now the signal is coming from the train station. Here—call Kathy, and then we'll head over to the train station."

After Mark called Kathy and let her know what was happening, he and Doug headed over to the train station.

They were almost there when Doug said, "I'll call again to see if Shelly can tell us where to look." He dialed his phone and was talking to her when they saw the sheriff's car coming in the opposite direction.

Doug suddenly turned to Mark, and in a loud voice said, "It's right in front of us?"

They both stopped and started to look around when the sheriff's car drove by.

Doug, who was still on the phone, said, "And now it's moving away."

Mark looked up and realized that it must be in the sheriff's car. Mark yelled, "It's in there!" as he pointed at the car headed downtown. He pointed his finger at Doug and said, "You really need to get a car!" and then smiled.

Doug yelled, "*Me*? I think *you* should be the one to get a car, Mr. I-don't-know-where-my-phone-is."

Mark laughed and said, "Let's go talk to the sheriff." With a big wave of his arm, they headed downtown.

*

The sheriff had called Chris's dad from the car, who was waiting for them when the officers pulled up to the station. The sheriff and deputy got out of the car, and the deputy opened the back door to let Chris out.

The sheriff walked over to Mr. McPhay and said, "Evening, Joe. Sorry to have to call you and all, but I think we have a problem. Let's step inside, shall we?"

Mr. McPhay said in a low voice as his son walked up to the front door, "What have you got me into this time?" He pulled his hand back like he was going to smack him and then stopped when he remembered where he was. He added, "Just wait until we get home."

The sheriff turned around when he saw what happened in the window reflection, and after letting Chris go inside, said, "Joe, I know about your trouble, but if I see one mark or even hear about what I think you're planning, I'll run you in so fast your head will spin. Clear?"

"Crystal," he said through a bit lip and took off his ball cap and slapped it into his other hand as he walked into the sheriff's building.

All four walked into the briefing room, which was also the lunch room, kitchen, gun cleaning, and interrogation room.

Everyone took a seat, and the sheriff said, "So what were you doing down at the train station today?"

Joe looked at Chris sternly and said, "You were at the train station? I was down there today waiting for someone, but I didn't see you there. And besides, I told you not to hang out there, didn't I?"

"If you don't mind, this is *my* investigation," the sheriff said to Joe. He looked back at Chris and said, "Well? What were you doing?"

Chris shifted in his seat as he looked down at the table. He looked up and said, "I was just there to use the restroom … honest. Me and Tommy were walking past, and I had to go to the bathroom really bad."

Then the sheriff pulled out the note in a plastic evidence bag and threw it on the table. He said, "Okay, Chris. Tell us about 'Operation Dog Water." The deputy, Mr. McPhay and Chris all looked at the sheriff like he was losing his mind. "Come, on. Tell us about it."

Chris said, "You mean about the bomb?"

His dad looked at him in shock. The deputy looked at him in surprise. The sheriff slammed his hands on the table and yelled, "Then you did know about it. Who's next?

Where are they hiding? How are they supposed to contact you? Did you already plant the bomb somewhere?"

"No, no, *no!* I don't know about any bomb."

"But you just said you knew about it," the sheriff said with a red face.

"When I was in the stall, you came into the bathroom at the train station today and said there was a bomb."

The room fell quiet. You could see the wheels turning as the sheriff recounted the day's events. Then he said, "I'll be right back," and he walked out of the room.

He walked into his office, closed the door. and sat at his desk. He walked through everything step by step, beginning with when he first he heard the news—the call from the mayor, the looking for signs of trouble with the deputy, the train station, and then the note. Then Chris had come running out of the restroom stall ... and then the phone ringing. His mind seemed to keep coming back to the train station. What was the connection?

"That's it! The train station is the connection!" he said. It hit him like a lightning bolt. He started to put all the pieces together. *The phone belongs to Mr. McPhay, not his son. Mr. McPhay was laid off from his contracting job that was repairing the train station about a year ago and hasn't been able find work since. Mr. McPhay admitted he was down at the train station* waiting *for someone.*

Now it was all starting to make sense. "I have proof of the evidence, motive, and opportunity." He thought about that for a moment and then brushed it off. "He has to be our man. Now I can call the Feds." And with that, in one smooth move, he pulled out his cell phone and hit the speed button for the FBI.

CHAPTER 17

Mark and Doug were just about to walk into the sheriff's office when Doug's phone rang. He told Mark to go ahead in and that he would follow in a second.

Doug answered the phone and said, "Oh, hi, sir. Yes, I'm in town." He listened to the speaker for a moment. "You want me to go to the sheriff's office to check out a claim on a terrorist act—in *this* town? I just happen to be working on … umm … something else that brought me there now. I'll find out what's going on and get back to you. Yes, sir. I do know who we are dealing with. Yes, sir, okay. Thank you, sir."

Doug entered the office and saw Mark sitting in a chair near the front desk. "What are you doing sitting there? I thought you were going to ask about your phone."

"The sheriff told me to take a seat and not make any noise while he interrogates his prisoner."

"His prisoner? What has he gotten himself into this time?" Doug asked as he walked toward the room with the closed door.

Mark said, "Be careful. He had a strange look about him. I mean, stranger than normal."

"Thanks," Doug said, reaching into his pocket as he opened the door.

The sheriff was standing over the table pointing his finger at Mr. McPhay, saying, "I got you dead to rights, and I can prove it."

Doug cleared his voice and closed the door. He said, "Evening, Sheriff. I got a call to come to talk to you. What have you got?"

"I didn't call you. I called the ..." He stopped when Doug pulled his hand out of his pocket with his FBI badge and flashed it him. The sheriff looked at the badge in disbelief and said in a low voice, "But I thought they were going to send the 'big boys.' Why are you here?"

"Around here, Henry, I *am* the big boy. Now tell me what you've got."

The sheriff got a little red in the face and then told his story. He started with when he talked with the mayor, how he instructed his deputy to take care of the paperwork, how he organized the searching of the town, and how he took it upon himself to check out the train station. Through his expert intuition, he said, he was able to utilize his detective skills and find the evidence the suspect had left behind. Through his professional investigational skills, he was able to track down the person he was charging now. "And I can prove without a reasonable doubt that Mr. Joe McPhay has not only planned the whole thing but was going to set off a bomb here in this town."

Mr. McPhay started to protest, but Doug waved his hand and stopped him from getting out of his seat. "And you can *prove* he was going to set off a bomb in *this town*, right?"

"Well ... umm ... maybe not conclusively prove, but I know he did it. He had motive and opportunity. Besides, I have his phone from the train station where he dropped this note." He handed Doug the plastic bag.

Doug looked at the piece of paper in the bag and smiled. He looked back at the sheriff and said, "Is this all you have? This piece of paper?"

The sheriff almost beamed and said, "No, I also have this." He walked over to a file cabinet, opened a drawer, and pulled out another plastic bag. "I have his phone, which his son has admitted losing at the train station."

"But that's not—" Again Mr. McPhay started to protest, and again Doug stopped him.

"Please, continue, Sheriff."

"Right … umm … oh, yeah. So this is the phone the boy lost at the train station. I haven't dusted it for prints yet, but I'm sure you will find the perp's prints all over it," the sheriff finished and then pulled up his pants by the belt and looked at the McPhays with a "so there" expression.

Doug looked at the paper and the phone and said, "I want to get a second opinion on this; just a minute." He walked over and opened the door. Mark was still sitting in the chair next to the desk, like some kid waiting to see the principal. Doug waved his hand and said, "Mark, would you mind coming in here for a moment?"

Everyone looked at each other in confusion.

Mark came in and Doug closed the door. He said, "Mark, do you know everyone in here?"

Mark looked around and said, "Yes, that's Joe. That's his son, Chris. That's Miles the deputy and Sheriff Strange." And as an afterthought, he smiled and said, "And you're my next-door neighbor. What's going on?"

"Yes, what is going on here, Mr. Agent Man?" the sheriff asked with a little impatience.

"Easy, Sheriff, you're already on thin ice. I'd hate to see you drown." He turned his attention back to Mark. "Mark, what else do you know about Joe, other than his being a safety inspector at your job?"

Mark looked down at the floor and said, "It was his truck that hit me when I was a kid."

Joe jumped up and said, "Is that what this is all about? Are you trying to set me up for something? I paid my debt to society, yet I was made the scapegoat for the construction accident. Someone brought in unchecked supplies without checking with me and—"

"Mr. McPhay, please sit down and not say another word. This man holds your future in his hands," Doug said, pointing at his chair.

Mr. McPhay closed his mouth and slowly sat.

Doug turned back to Mark and said, "And as a result of the accident, what happened?"

"I lost my short-term memory and have to write things down," he said quietly.

Doug said, "What's that in your shirt pocket?"

Mark reached up and pulled out his notebook. "It's my 'virtual memory,' so I don't forget things."

"Like what?" Doug continued.

"Pretty much anything I have to do that day."

"So what kind of things do you have to remember? Do you have to remember to … I don't know … get out of bed? Do you have to remember to … eat a meal?"

"No, it's not like that. I write down things, like, to remember to bring things home, to pick up something from the store, dinner dates … which we are late for. Or to take care of our pet."

"Oh, so you have a pet? What kind do you have?"

"A dog. It's pretty old, and I have to remember to pick up medicine for it, or sometimes to give it something to drink."

"So you write these things down in your 'virtual memory,' do you? Do you ever take out a piece of paper from the book?"

"As a habit, I try not to. But there have been times that I have. Why?"

Doug smiled a little and said, "May I see your book?"

Mark handed it to Doug.

"Did you recently rip out part of a page?" he asked as he tapped the book against his hand.

Mark said, "I think so. Wait, today, to give Brian my phone number."

"Would you turn to the page you ripped it from?" Doug handed the book back to Mark and looked around the room like a magician performing an act.

Mark opened the book to the last page and handed it back to Doug. Doug picked up the piece of paper still in the plastic bag in one hand and held the open book in the other so everyone could see that it matched.

Doug asked Mark, "So, your *dog* needs an operation. What kind?"

Mark said, "He needs to have his hips readjusted. I've been told its pretty common in this breed."

"And you wrote something about 'water.' What's that for?"

Mark looked back down to the floor and said, "Sometimes I forget to give the dog water, so I wrote it down so I didn't forget this time." He thought about it and looked back up at everyone and said reassuringly, "And I did remember."

The sheriff froze. Then he said, "But I have Joe's phone. I can still get a conviction on that."

Doug picked up the phone, still in its bag, and said, "Mark, does this look familiar?"

Mark said in a loud voice, "You found my phone! But why is it in a plastic bag?"

"You might want to ask the sheriff," Doug said, looking over in his direction.

The sheriff rolled his eyes, gave a little cough, and in a rough, low voice said, "Joe, you're free to go, with the apologies of this office. I'll understand if you wish to make a formal complaint with the mayor's office."

"I just might do that, Sheriff. I just might do that."

Doug stopped Mr. McPhay from walking out the door and said, "Joe, I know things haven't been so good lately, but please think about bringing up charges. I'm not telling *not* to file, but just think of those who really have it worse than you."

"Yeah, yeah … I'll think about it," Joe said as he put on his cap and walked out the door, pushing Chris into the lead.

Then Doug turned to Mark and said, "Would you and Miles please wait for me outside a minute? I have to have a word with the sheriff."

"Yeah, sure." Mark looked at the sheriff, who was standing there with his head hung down, and said, "I'll be just outside … umm … waiting."

Deputy Miles stuck his hands in his pockets and looked down, and with a quick step, he followed Mark out the door.

It was almost seven o'clock. Mark and the deputy were standing around the front desk, and the phone rang.

Just as the deputy answered it, Doug came out, and Mark asked, "Well, what happened?"

The sheriff came out, still looking down, and mumbled, "What a day. I'm glad it's over."

The deputy covered the receiver and said "Umm … Sheriff? It's the commissioner. He wants to talk to you."

The sheriff took in a deep breath and slowly exhaled.

Doug looked at Mark and said, "We'd better go."

Outside, Mark again said, "Tell me what happened."

Doug looked up and down the sidewalk to see if anyone was around and murmured, "Can you keep a secret?"

Mark, thinking this was going to be good, said, "Yeah, you know I can."

Doug motioned him to come closer and then looked around one more time and said, "So can I."

"Oh, you're so funny I forgot to laugh."

"Yeah, I know," Doug said with a silly grin. "I have that effect on people."

"Uh-huh, right. Let's go, Chuckles, I do believe we were supposed to go to *your* house for my birthday dinner."

"Hey, that was good. You didn't even have to look at your book to remember that it was your birthday, did you?"

"When it comes to food, my memory gets better. By the way, did you pick up my phone? I have to call Kathy to let her know we're on the way."

"Here you go. And tell her to keep the dog at home this time. I don't want it dropping dead in my house."

"Our dog has more class than to kick the bucket at your place."

"This coming from the guy who still uses a Fred and Barney breakfast set to eat his cereal in the morning. I think I'm going to have to call—what's his name—Bill, to compare notes with."

"For your information, that breakfast set is a collector's item, and as far as *Brian* is concerned ..."

As the two men walked down the sidewalk, their voices trailed off and started to mix with the sounds of the busy street of their hometown.

CHAPTER 18

At the birthday party, both Doug and Mark showed up a bit late but made up for it by telling everyone about their day. Brian stopped by for a few hours to catch up with Mark and Kathy and was able to share stories with Doug.

The next day all returned to normal. Mark continued to write things in his "visual memory," but he never again ripped out a page or even a small corner ever again. Doug had to report to the main office on the events of the day before.

And down at the sheriff's office, things were a little different. A new sheriff sat reading the newspaper with his feet up on the desk. Henry Strange, now Deputy Strange, emerged from one of the jail cells and said, "Okay, I've cleaned all the cells. What else do you want me to do?"

"You forgot the magic word, Deputy."

"Are you really going to make me say it?" Strange asked, looking at the floor.

"You betcha," said the sheriff, putting down the newspaper and smiling. The new sheriff was none other than Miles Frederickson. It seemed Miles had been doing some home schooling for the past few years and passed his courses with flying colors. The commissioner was so impressed with his final exam scores that he made him the new sheriff. "Come on, the magic word …"

"What else do you want me to do, *sir*?"

"Ahhh, music to my ears. I think I'm ready for lunch." The new sheriff smiled and went back to his paper.